HEDGEHOGS IN THE HALL

Mandy Hope loves animals more than anything else. She knows quite a lot about them too: both her parents are vets and Mandy helps out in their surgery, Animal Ark. Rescuing an injured mother hedgehog is difficult enough—but what will happen to her terrified babies? Who will look after them? There's no room at Animal Ark for wild animals. Can Mandy and James safely release the hedgehog family back into the wild?

HEDGEHOGS IN THE HALL

Lucy Daniels

Galaxy

CHIVERS PRESS
BATH

First published 1994
by
Knight Books
This Large Print edition published by
Chivers Press
by arrangement with
Hodder Children's Books
2000

ISBN 0 7540 6109 4

Special thanks to Jenny Oldfield for all
her help and also to C.J. Hall,
B.Vet.Med., MRCVS

British Library Cataloguing in Publication Data

Daniels, Lucy
  Hedgehogs in the hall.—Large print ed.
  1. Animal Ark (Imaginary place)—Juvenile fiction
  2. Hedgehogs—Juvenile fiction 3. Children's stories 4. Large type
      books
  I. Title
  823.9'14[J]

ISBN 0-7540-6109-4

Printed and bound in Great Britain by
REDWOOD BOOKS, Trowbridge, Wiltshire

To Fiona Waters, who showed me my first hedgehog.

CHAPTER ONE

'Watch out, you two!' Mr Hunter warned.

Mandy and James jumped well out of the way of the garden mower. James's dad had almost finished cutting the grass, a job he disliked. James had been helping by raking up leaves when Mandy arrived, and the two of them decided to join in the garden chores together. Autumn smells of wet earth and leaf mould drifted in the air. It would soon be Bonfire Night.

'Watch out!' Mr Hunter yelled again. He stomped past, carrying a heavy load of grass clippings for the compost heap.

James and Mandy followed him up the garden with armfuls of brown leaves.

'Whoa!' he said. He sprinkled the grass on to the compost. 'Drop that lot over there!' He pointed with his garden fork to another corner, under a beech tree. Then he plunged the fork deep into the compost.

1

Mandy let the leaves fall in the damp shade of the beech tree. She glanced up and saw James's new neighbour, a girl of about eight, peering silently over the hedge at them. 'Hi!' she said, cheerfully brushing leaves off the front of her jumper. 'I'm Mandy Hope from Animal Ark.' She remembered that the little girl had already been into the surgery with her pet rabbit. It wasn't eating properly. The move to a new house must have upset it. 'How's your rabbit?' Mandy asked.

But the girl didn't answer. Instead, her pale, staring face with its huge, dark eyes and frame of dark, straight hair, bobbed down behind the hedge without even a smile.

'What did I say?' Mandy wondered.

James shook his head. 'Don't ask me. I asked her over to visit yesterday. Mum said I had to. She did the same thing to me—just stared and vanished!'

'Hmm.' Mandy frowned. The girl couldn't be all bad. After all, they had something in common: they both had pet rabbits! 'What's her name?'

James finished piling up the leaves

2

and brushed his hands against each other. 'Claire something. She's the new doctor's daughter. I don't know.' He lost interest and went to rake up more leaves.

'Good Lord!' A sudden shout went up from Mr Hunter over by the compost heap.

Mandy sprinted over. James's dad stood, garden fork poised in mid-air. James ran up the length of the lawn to see what the fuss was about.

'Look!' Mr Hunter jabbed downwards with his fork. A large, round bundle of leaves, straw and scraps of newspaper rolled slowly on to the edge of the lawn. 'It's moving!' Mr Hunter cried. 'It's moving all by itself!'

Mandy gasped. The bundle, about the size of a football, was in fact rocking and trundling forward of its own accord. 'Don't touch it!' she said. She pulled at James's sleeve.

'What is it?' he said.

'Shh!' Mandy held up her hand.

Even Mr Hunter lowered his voice. 'I just stuck my fork into the bottom of the heap there, and hey presto, out

3

came this thing on the end of it!' he whispered. 'What on earth's happening?'

'I'm not sure. Wait a moment!' Mandy crouched down beside the moving ball. She was sure her father had shown her one like this before, only not quite so big. It was in a hedge in their own garden at Animal Ark. 'I think it's a hedgehog's nest! Look!'

And sure enough, a long snout emerged from the ball and sniffed the air, followed by two dark, bright eyes, a pair of small, furry ears and two front paws complete with five sharp claws. Half in, half out of its nest, the hedgehog blinked at the daylight.

Mr Hunter, who liked gardening because it gave him a break from his work in the insurance office, leaned on his garden fork for support. 'I could've put a spike straight through that little chap!' he said, breathing a sigh of relief.

'Hang on!' Mandy knelt on all fours. James crouched beside her. The hedgehog was scrambling free of the disturbed nest. Its plump little body

4

squeezed out between a gap in the interwoven wall. It half fell, rolled into a spiky ball, then landed on firm ground. 'It's not a chap!' Mandy whispered. 'Look!'

Four more tiny, dark noses followed. Four more pairs of front feet. Four miniature balls covered in pale fawn spikes tumbled out of the nest on to the grass.

'It's a mother hedgehog!' Mandy cried. 'And her babies!'

Mr Hunter wiped his forehead with the sleeve of his sweater. 'A narrow escape!' he breathed. 'Are they all right?'

'I think so.' Mandy had recovered from her surprise. 'I think they must like compost heaps for their nurseries. Loads of maggots and worms and things to eat.'

'Yuck!' James shuddered. He watched the mother unroll herself, sniffing, snorting and puffing herself up to take on any enemy. The babies unrolled too and queued up behind her in single file.

'They don't like the daylight though,'

Mandy said, worried again.

'What shall we do?' Mr Hunter asked. He bent down as if to shoo the mother hedgehog back into the compost heap.

'No, I don't think that's any good. We'd better leave them.' Mandy knew not to interfere with a mother and her babies. 'If the mother's still nursing the little ones and we get in the way now, she's likely to turn round and destroy them!' Mr Hunter and James looked shocked.

'What, she'd kill her own young?' James said, open-mouthed.

Mandy nodded. 'Or else she'd just desert them. And that comes to the same thing. Without her, they'd soon die!'

Since Mr Hope had shown Mandy her first hedgehog's nest, she'd been reading a booklet on the little creatures, not guessing how soon it would come in useful.

The three humans squatted on the edge of the lawn as the hedgehog family sniffed and snuffled to get their bearings. James and Mr Hunter waited

6

for Mandy to decide what to do.

'She's probably got another nest somewhere nearby. They usually have half a dozen or so. Let's wait for her to find a safe one.' She sounded confident, but Mandy knew these little creatures only came out at night. Daytime smells, sights and sounds could easily confuse them.

They waited. The mother hedgehog sniffed the misty air. Her eyesight was poor, but she made up for it with a sharp sense of smell, according to the booklet. Soon the mother set off, zigzagging up the lawn, her babies close behind. They headed for wide open space, in the opposite direction to the hedge, their natural home.

'They're lost!' James whispered.

Mandy nodded. 'Afraid so. It's the daylight that's throwing them off course, but there's nothing we can do. Except keep watch!'

'They're heading for the house!' Mr Hunter groaned.

The miniature procession didn't swerve or falter now. It headed down the side of the house, straight for the

7

chrysanthemum tub outside the Hunters' front door. Mandy, James and Mr Hunter followed at a safe distance.

'Maybe she'll find out she's going the wrong way!' James said, trying to be positive. 'They sure move fast, don't they?' The little hedgehog family had covered one hundred metres of lawn in double-quick time. Now they scuttled in circles in the area of the Hunters' front door.

Then up they went on to the first stone step, heads raised, sniffing the air, even the little ones! And up again in bold procession, mother and four babies, up the next step into the Hunters' hallway!

'They've gone inside the house!' James breathed. 'They're in the hall!'

'Hedgehogs in the hall!' Mr Hunter gulped.

'They're all covered in fleas and things, aren't they? Your mother will have a fit!'

Mandy tried to hold him back while the hedgehogs realised their mistake. But Mr Hunter had panicked.

'Chrissie!' he yelled to his wife somewhere inside the house. The hedgehog procession halted, perhaps puzzled by the feel of the hall carpet, the smells of polish and air freshener.

'Ye-es!' Mrs Hunter sang out from the kitchen.

'Don't come into the hall!' Mr Hunter warned.

But of course, that's what she did! 'What do you mean, don't come into the hall?' she demanded, opening the glass panelled kitchen door.

There was a bouncing, scrambling, scrabbling noise behind her; a large animal sound.

'Blackie!' It was James's Labrador, and James was first to realise the dangers. He shot up the steps into the hall, past the family of refugee hedgehogs. He wanted to grab Blackie before the dog pushed past Mrs Hunter and bounded down the hallway. A black Labrador's soft nose was no match for an angry hedgehog's spines. James lunged for the dog—and missed! 'What on earth's going on?' Mrs Hunter demanded.

Mandy too shot up the steps into the hall, to stand between Blackie and the hedgehogs. 'Down, Blackie! Stay down!' she commanded.

But the dog took no notice. He'd spotted uninvited guests. It was too late to stop him. He took three bounds and crouched, nose to nose with the mother hedgehog!

'Blackie, don't!' James cried.

They stood helpless. The hedgehog tucked her nose under her and flexed her backbone. She turned into a ball of strong, sharp spikes; thousands of them. The tiny babies followed suit. The dog growled. He kept his nose to the ground and bared his teeth. He snapped and lunged. Then he leapt back, yelping and whining. He almost felled Mandy, who stood there in the hall, helpless. Blackie recoiled in pain and anger from the hedgehog's dangerous spikes.

As the dog howled and retreated into the kitchen, the hedgehog made her getaway. Instantly she unrolled and was back on her feet. She was down the hallway before Mandy had time to think. Someone had already locked the wounded Blackie in the kitchen and the four little hedgehogs remained curled up on the carpet. They were probably petrified! But the mother was off!

Out of the house, past James's puzzled cat, Eric, down the steps, along the front path, scuttling at top speed!

'Stop her!' Mandy shouted at Mr Hunter. He stood astride the path between hedgehog and freedom. 'She's heading for the road! Stop her!'

'How?' Mr Hunter looked bewildered. Like Mandy, he thought too slowly to act. The hedgehog dashed past.

Mandy watched the terrified creature bolt for the gate. She glanced down at the four babies, still tightly rolled and frozen to the spot in the Hunters' hallway. Then she ran after the mother.

The hedgehog had reached the garden gate. It was closed, but she shot straight under it. Too frightened to sense danger, she ran out into the road.

Mandy could hear a car coming. She

flung open the gate. There was a screech of brakes. She heard it and couldn't bear to look. One hand went up to her eyes. The mother hedgehog had fled out of the Hunters' garden, straight under the wheels of a car!

CHAPTER TWO

The accident was so sudden and quick that it was over before Mandy really knew what had happened.

The car brakes screeched and skidded. The engine cut out. Then silence!

Mandy uncovered her eyes. 'Let her be all right!' she breathed. 'Oh, please let her be alive!'

The car was slewed sideways, its nose pointed into the ditch on the far side of the road. It had stayed upright and in one piece, however. It was a big, silver car with mud spattered all along its side from the skid. A man opened the driver's door and stepped out on to the road. He was shaking his head.

12

'Did I hit it?' he asked anxiously. He was a tall, dark-haired man in a dark grey suit.

'I don't know!' Mandy cried. 'Where is she? I can't see her!' She looked wildly up and down the stretch of road.

'There!' The man pointed to the gutter by Mandy's feet. He pronounced the 'r' with a long Scottish roll.

Her heart sank. The hedgehog hadn't escaped the car wheels. She bent down to look, expecting the worst.

The mother hedgehog was curled in a tight ball, but one dark leg stuck out straight at an odd angle. There was no sound from the small creature.

'Oh!' Mandy half sobbed. 'She's hurt!'

'But alive,' the man said, bending down alongside Mandy. 'Her leg's broken, I think.'

'Poor thing!' Mandy exclaimed in a quiet voice. She looked down at the victim and began to get her thoughts in order. She was over the shock. Now she hoped she could save the hedgehog, and there was lots to do.

She went back to fetch the thick

13

leather gardening gloves which Mr Hunter always had stuffed into his waistcoat pocket, then she thrust her hands deep inside. 'There,' she said, gently beginning to talk as she rescued the hedgehog from the gutter. 'There, there, we'll look after you!' Slowly she slid a gloved hand under the tight ball. 'I want to get her away from the road,' she told the man. Gently she lifted the hedgehog, rocking her in the palm of the glove as she did so.

The man looked at Mandy and nodded. 'I'll straighten up my car,' he said. 'In fact, I'll drive it into my driveway. I live just next door. You can follow me!'

Mandy looked surprised. 'Next door?' In the house with the unfriendly girl?

He had one leg inside the car, one hand on the steering wheel. 'Yes, I'm a doctor. And you seem to know about animals. Between us we should be able to manage this!' He smiled, then he eased the car straight on the road. He drove it slowly down his own drive.

Mandy continued to think quickly.

14

She glanced up the path to the Hunters' house. They were still inside, probably looking after poor Blackie and the baby hedgehogs. It would be better if she went with the doctor to his house to tend to the injured mother. She ran carefully down next door's drive, cradling the hedgehog in the giant gloves.

The same dark haired girl as before appeared silently from behind a pile of wood for the bonfire she was building at the bottom of the garden. Her father waved briefly at her but she didn't wave back. When she saw Mandy running anxiously into the house after him, she just stared and withdrew again into the shadow of the huge stack of wood.

'Quick, come into the kitchen. My wife's here. She'll be able to help,' the doctor said.

'I've run over a hedgehog,' he explained to the small, sandy-haired woman who met them at the kitchen door. 'Would you boil some water for us and fill a hot-water bottle? Then wrap it in a towel. The hedgehog's suffering from shock, so we've got to

15

keep up its body heat!' He moved quickly, spreading clean tea towels on the table. 'Now,' he said, 'how do we unroll the poor wee thing?'

'I know how!' Mandy told him. She liked this man; his promptness, his Scottish accent. 'I live at Animal Ark,' she explained. 'My mum and dad are both vets. I'm Mandy Hope.'

'And I'm David McKay,' he said, shaking her free hand. 'Now I'll fetch the disinfectant from our first-aid box, in case there's any wound to wash down, while you have a go at unrolling her, OK?'

Mandy knew from Simon, the nurse at Animal Ark, that if you rocked a hedgehog gently back and forth, the movement would gradually make it unflex its spine. She began rocking, talking softly, while Mrs McKay came up with the wrapped hot-water bottle. Slowly the hedgehog let itself unroll, revealing a soft, browny-grey belly and one back leg completely dislocated. It still stuck out at an odd angle, broken and useless. Halfway down the dark leg, well above the little clawed foot, was an open red wound.

'Hmm . . .' Dr McKay frowned. 'We'd best bathe that with the warm disinfectant.' He gave Mandy a swab of cotton-wool dipped in the diluted mixture. 'I'll sort out a shot of antibiotic for her. Back in a tick.'

His wife stood by and watched as Mandy gently bathed and cleansed the wound. The little hedgehog sniffed and trembled, but didn't roll back up into a spiky ball. She let Mandy treat the injury.

Then Dr McKay came back and skilfully injected a small dose of antibiotic. 'Lucky, really,' he said. 'If you have to be a hedgehog who's run over, who better to rescue you than a vet's daughter?' He smiled at Mandy.

'Here's a nice, deep cardboard box,' Mrs McKay said, fishing for one in a cupboard under the sink. She put the hot-water bottle in it, amongst some loose newspaper scrunched up in the bottom. 'Now what still needs to be done?'

The wound seemed clean at last. Mandy discarded the cotton-wool swab and lowered the mother hedgehog into the warm nest. 'I need to take her back to Animal Ark,' she said, 'so we can set the broken bone.' She looked gratefully at Dr and Mrs McKay. 'I'd better go and let the Hunters know.' She picked up the box with the hedgehog nestled comfortably inside. Then another thought struck her.

'The babies!' She had last seen them in the Hunters' hallway. 'And Blackie! I'd better go!' Hurriedly she went to the front door. 'Thanks! I'm sorry I have to rush!'

Dr McKay nodded in his brisk, busy way. 'Not at all. I'm only sorry I was the cause of all this. I'll have to take more care in future!'

'I'm glad you swerved,' Mandy told him. 'Lots of people wouldn't have bothered.' She gave him a quick smile and went off down the drive. Then she nipped quickly back up the path to the Hunters' house.

'James!' she called. 'Is Blackie OK?' She stood on the doorstep with her cardboard box, anxious to keep the hedgehog out of harm's way.

James came out, slightly pale, but calm. He nodded. 'He's OK now. His nose bled like mad at first, but my mum washed it all off and disinfected it.'

'And the baby hedgehogs? What about them?'

James shook his head. 'I don't know. I'm sorry; we were so busy with Blackie I forgot to check,' he admitted.

Mandy looked down the empty hallway, then scanned the garden and down the side of the house. The babies had vanished.

'They're too small to manage alone!' she told James. 'They need their mother!'

'But you said the mother wouldn't have anything to do with them now!' James had come out into the garden to join in the search. He looked behind the flower-tub and along the lawn.

'Not if we have to handle them,' Mandy agreed. Then she had an idea. 'Look after the mother, will you, please?' she asked James. She handed the box to him. 'Her leg's broken. I've got to get her to Animal Ark.' But first she sprinted to the far hedge to pick up the empty hedgehog nest still lying by the compost heap. 'If we find the babies, maybe we can get them to crawl back in here,' she explained.

'Now what?' Mr Hunter peered out of the kitchen, one hand firmly on Blackie's collar. He'd taken off his gardening boots and stood there in big woollen socks. 'How's the other patient?' He pointed to the box. 'Still alive?'

Mandy nodded and explained again. But they were losing precious time. 'It's the babies we're worried about now. Do you know what happened to them, Mr Hunter?'

He thought for a few moments. 'Now, let's see. They were last seen in the hall here; four little spiky balls. One whimpering dog in the kitchen causing much chaos.' He scratched his head. 'Oh, now I remember! The four little balls unrolled, headed straight for the fresh air, after their mother. Didn't go off down the path kamikaze style like Mum, though. No, I think they took a sharp left by the flower-tub.

They headed back where they came from!'

Mandy nodded. 'Thanks!' She scouted off down the side of the house, calling and peering under every bush. Under her arm she held the closely woven nest of twigs and leaves. She stooped low, studied the ground beneath the hedge, trying to find anything that looked like hedgehog runs. These were the tracks they wore through grass and leaves during their regular nightly visits. They were a sure sign of hedgehogs in any garden.

But she came face to face not with hedgehogs, but with the McKay girl. Again! The pale face stared back at her from ground level. Mandy stared back at the serious blank face. 'Do you know where the baby hedgehogs went?' she whispered.

The girl nodded slowly.

'Where?' Mandy gasped.

'They're in my bonfire!' she announced. She said 'my' defiantly. 'They ran in there to hide!'

Mandy nodded. Of course; it was another good place for hedgehogs, full of insects and beetles! 'Wait there!' she said. She had to be careful not to upset Claire. 'I'll bring their nest round and try and coax them out again. But don't touch them, OK? Just keep an eye on them!' She knew how vital it was to get the mother and babies back together without putting the scent of humans on them.

The girl vanished from the other side of the hedge, her face still pale and sulky.

'Remember, don't touch the babies!' Mandy repeated. She scrambled to her feet, grabbed the empty nest from the Hunters' lawn and sprinted along the length of the hedge to the front gate. She was up into the lane and down the McKays' drive, carrying the empty nest.

She headed for the half-built bonfire, making plans to rescue the whole family and take it back to Animal Ark. They would be able to look after them all and keep them with the mother. Mandy had it all worked out. She would coax the babies back into the nest with fresh worms or some other tasty morsel. They would be hungry. She hoped they would fall for her trick.

She ran as fast as she could. But it was already too late.

Claire stood there guarding her woodpile. She was holding a shallow plastic laundry basket. She held it up as Mandy arrived. 'I rescued them!' she announced, shoving the basket under Mandy's nose. 'I grabbed them before they could burrow further into the bonfire, see!'

Mandy looked into the basket. Inside the bare, white plastic container four little hedgehogs scrabbled and fought to escape. Their claws slipped on the shiny surface. They cried and called out in panic.

Mandy closed her eyes and groaned. 'I said, don't touch them!' she sighed.

Claire stared back, hugging the basket close to her body. 'You can't tell me what to do!' she retorted. 'They're not yours!'

Inside the basket the babies slid and squealed. 'No, of course they're not,' Mandy agreed, taking a deep breath. 'But they needed their mother!' She

23

looked desperately at the girl. 'And now they need some proper extra care. We'll have to hand rear them!' It wasn't as good as she'd hoped for, but it was the best she could do. 'Please give them to me!' She put down the useless nest and held out her hands.

Claire stared back from beneath her dark fringe. Something wicked seemed to have got hold of her. She kept the basket clutched close to her. 'They're mine!' she said. 'I can look after them!' And swiftly she turned on her heel, and headed across the lawn towards the wide-open garage doors.

Mandy stood speechless. She watched the girl disappear into the garage with the four distressed babies. Claire had snatched them from their mother! She'd just turned all four of them into orphans!

Tears of anger stung her eyes as slowly she made her way back on to the road. James was there, silently watching. He handed over the mother hedgehog in her temporary bed without a word.

'I'd better get her home as soon as

possible,' Mandy said quietly. 'Did you see what happened?'

James nodded. 'I'll keep an eye on her,' he promised. 'Try not to worry.'

Mandy swallowed hard. She set off up the road into the village, carrying her patient with great care. Her heart felt heavy and her eyes were still hot with unshed tears when she reached her own gate and the wooden sign swinging in the breeze. 'Animal Ark, Veterinary Surgeon,' it said.

At least one hedgehog had reached safety, she told herself. She would have to be content with that.

CHAPTER THREE

'What have we here?' Jean Knox, the receptionist at Animal Ark, asked from behind her desk. 'Fish or fowl?'

Mandy gave her a weak smile. 'Neither. It's a hedgehog.' She set the box down on Jean's desk. 'Her leg's broken. We'll have to set it.'

Jean put on her glasses, which hung

on a chain round her neck, and peered into the box. She noticed the hot-water bottle. 'I see you've already given her some first-aid.' She looked closely at Mandy. 'What's wrong? You seem upset.'

Mandy shook her head. 'Nothing. Who's on duty?' she asked. 'I'd like to get her seen to straight away. The poor thing's in pain.' The mother hedgehog wasn't moving; she lay quietly, her damaged leg hanging limp and useless.

Jean raised a section of the counter to let Mandy through into the treatment room. 'Simon's here. Your father's out at a conference in York and your mum had to go out on a call.' She opened the door for Mandy. 'A road accident victim by the look of things,' she told Simon. And she closed the door softly.

Simon was the nurse at Animal Ark. He'd only recently left college and still looked a bit like a student with his round glasses and serious face. But he was very good with animals, gentle and sure at the same time.

Mandy explained everything to him.

She'd kept Mr Hunter's gardening gloves in a corner of the box. She used them now to cradle the hedgehog and lift it out.

Simon nodded. He never said much, but he took everything in. He gently examined the wound. 'Nicely cleaned up!' he said. 'Did you give her water and glucose at the doctor's house?'

Mandy shook her head and went quickly for the glucose solution. She knew it was to help the animal recover from shock. She'd seen Simon treat small accident victims many times before. Sometimes it was hedgehogs like this one, or else stoats and weasels caught in traps. She loved the careful way he handled these tiny creatures.

She watched as he dripped the liquid from a narrow tube into the side of the hedgehog's mouth. Then he turned back to the broken leg. 'Look,' he said. 'The bone's just pierced the skin here. But it's a clean break. No need to X-ray.' He reached for a thin, perforated dressing. 'It's a simple fracture of the tibia. We can't use plaster of Paris straight away, just tape and a splint to hold the leg in place.

Efficiently, Mandy went for the tape and returned in time for Simon to fix the filmy wrapping into place with a sturdy strip of tape and plastic splints.

'Good,' Simon said, working quickly, with plenty of skill. Soon he had the injured back leg held firmly in place by stiff white splints. 'There, that should hold it still!' he said, standing back from the treatment table to admire their work.

Mandy couldn't help but smile at the forlorn little hedgehog with its stiff leg. She softly stroked its spines with her gloved hand. 'You look as if you've been in the wars!' she murmured.

'She has,' Simon agreed. 'But she should be fine now. And just to make sure . . .' He went across to another drawer, and with a flourish drew out a small drum of powder and a brush. He came back for one final treatment: 'A quick dust down with the anti-maggot powder!' he announced.

Even Mandy pulled a face,

'Nature's way!' Simon said brightly. 'Hedgehogs make wonderful homes for maggots, in-between those dangerous spines. And for fleas! Now the fleas are no problem; they won't jump off a hedgehog's back on to a human, so no worries! But maggots do carry infection, especially if there's a wound. It's nasty. So, lo and behold, one maggot-free hedgehog!' He finished dusting and once again he stood back from his patient. 'What will you call her?' he asked.

Mandy gazed at the sharp, knowing face, the inquisitive nose. She wanted a name that showed how hedgehogs roamed the countryside, little free spirits. 'Rosa!' she said. That was a gypsy name and it suited the little traveller. She scooped her up and back into the warm, home-made nest. 'What will she need to eat?'

'Toads, worms, caterpillars, earwigs, slugs, dead mice, birds . . .' Simon reeled off a long list, then laughed at Mandy's horrified face. 'Or else cat food!' he suggested. 'That would be considered five star food by any hedgehog!'

'Phew, thank heavens!' Mandy said,

with something more like her usual grin. Simon might look serious and studious with his short, fair hair and round-rimmed glasses, but he was always joking and teasing. 'What about bread and milk?' she asked.

'No, not really.' Simon cleared the table and disinfected it. 'Cows' milk contains bacteria which are bad for hedgehogs. I know people like to leave out dishes of milk for them, but I wouldn't recommend it myself. Water's better.' He wiped his hands dry on a paper towel.

Mandy nodded and made a mental note of everything. She was determined that Rosa would get the very best care.

'She'll be fine,' Simon reassured her again.

Mandy nodded. 'Thanks to you!'

'So what's the matter?' Simon asked gently. 'Why do you still look down in the dumps?'

Mandy stared down into Rosa's box. At last she brought herself to explain. 'Rosa's got four babies!' she said, shaking her head. 'I tried to rescue them too, but someone else decided they could do it better!'

'Who?' Simon asked quietly.

'Claire McKay!' Mandy spoke more loudly than she intended. And all her worries about the baby hedgehogs came tumbling out. 'They're so tiny!' she said.

Simon nodded. 'They're called piglets. I don't suppose they're weaned from their mother's milk yet, otherwise they wouldn't still be in the nest, would they?'

Mandy shook her head. 'So what will they do now?' she asked, desperation in her eyes.

Simon looked quickly at his watch. 'Well, we've finished surgery here,' he said. 'How about if we leave a message with Jean for your mother, and then I can come down with you to Claire's house?'

Mandy looked up at him with sudden hope. 'Would you?' she said. Her eyes brightened at the idea.

'Of course! Even if we can't persuade Claire to give us the piglets to look after, at least we can give her some good tips on hedgehog care!'

Simon smiled and placed Rosa's box under the warm light of an incubator. 'It's worth a visit, wouldn't you say?'

Mandy felt a heavy weight beginning to lift. 'Why didn't I think of that?'

'Because you were worried stiff about four helpless little babies adrift in the wide world without their mother,' he said simply. 'It's understandable.'

Mandy nodded, smiled and heaved a huge sigh of relief.

So they set off together in Simon's battered old van. They rattled over the back lanes towards the road where the Hunters and the McKays lived.

*   *   *

Mandy rang the McKays' front doorbell with a trembling hand. She was glad Simon was standing there with her in the gathering dusk. She pulled her woollen scarf closer round her chin. They waited.

A light went on in the hall, then the door opened. Claire McKay stood, one hand raised and resting on the latch.

She didn't speak.

'Hello!' Mandy tried to sound cheerful. 'There's good news about the mother hedgehog. She's going to be all right! We thought you'd like to know.'

Still there was no reaction from Claire.

'How are her babies?' Mandy asked. 'I've brought Simon along just to check they're OK. Simon's the nurse at Animal Ark.'

Still no reply. Then Claire must have heard a movement behind her, from down the hallway. She moved as if to close the door. 'They're mine!' she said finally. 'No one else can look at them!'

'Claire!' Mrs McKay's light, soft voice floated down the hall. 'Who's at the door?' She sounded anxious, but she relaxed when she saw Mandy. 'Well, hello again!' she said to her. 'You must be freezing standing out there in the cold! Come on in!'

Claire scowled, but they accepted. If Mrs McKay could help keep Claire calm, Mandy realised they would have more chance of getting to the piglets. So, in the warmth of the kitchen,

33

Mandy introduced Simon to Dr and Mrs McKay.

'How's the wee hedgehog?' Mrs McKay asked, offering them tea and special flat griddle scones with butter and jam.

'On the mend,' Simon said. He described Rosa's injuries.

Things were going well, Mandy thought. Everyone was friendly and concerned—except the dreadful Claire. She sat in a corner, angry and silent.

'Claire, why don't you take Mandy to see your pet rabbit,' Dr McKay suggested after a long look in his daughter's direction. 'We'll finish our tea here.'

There was something clear and firm in his voice which even sulky Claire couldn't ignore. She stared back at him for a second, then turned and swung open a side door. It connected the house to the garage via a glass-roofed corridor which the McKays used as a laundry-room. Mandy peered through the door then looked back at Simon. He gave her an encouraging nod. 'You can sort her out,' he seemed to say. So

Mandy followed the younger girl.

Claire squatted beside a wooden hutch. She lightly ran her forefinger along the netting and gave Mandy one sly, sideways glance. Then she set her face, blank and stubborn as ever, back towards the rabbit in its hutch.

'What's his name?' Mandy asked calmly. She watched the bright-eyed little black rabbit emerge from his sleeping quarters.

'Sooty,' Claire answered quietly, almost swallowing the word.

'Nice name,' Mandy said. 'I have some pet rabbits at Animal Ark. Do you want to come and see them?'

Claire ignored the invitation, so Mandy took a dandelion leaf from a small pile on the floor and held it against the netting of the cage. Sooty sniffed, came forward and nibbled warily. 'How old is he?'

'Six months. He was only three months old when we came. Now he's six!'

'And is he eating his food properly?'

Claire nodded. 'He likes it here now.'

'But you don't?' Mandy guessed. She thought she'd put her finger on something important. Still she had to be very careful with Claire. It was just like talking to a wild rabbit who would bolt at the first false move.

Claire shook her head. 'I liked my old house. And my old school!'

Mandy got close enough to Sooty to tickle his nose. She smiled. 'It takes a while to settle in,' she agreed. She remembered how nasty Susan Collins had been when she first moved into the area. All because she was unhappy that her mother had stayed in London to work.

'Everything's different!' Claire wailed. 'Nobody's my friend!'

'Is that why you want to look after Rosa's babies?' Mandy asked. She looked again at this strange, lonely girl. She wanted the baby hedgehogs to be 'hers' because she had no one to talk to, because she didn't fit in!

Claire blushed, nodded and ducked her head. 'Maybe,' she admitted.

'Well, will you let me be your friend?' Mandy asked.

Again Claire stared back without answering.

'At least let us help,' Mandy offered gently. The laundry-room was full of packing-cases and spare furniture. She looked round at all the chaos of moving house. But where was the side door into the garage? Although Mandy was beginning to feel sorry for Claire, she was still keen to get to those tiny babies.

Claire considered things carefully. She sighed.

'Simon knows all about hedgehogs; what they eat, how soon they can look after themselves, everything! He can help you take care of Rosa's babies!' Mandy said again.

Claire sighed one last time and stood up. 'OK,' she said. 'Tell him he can come and take a look!'

Mandy grinned, nodded and dashed back into the kitchen. She told Simon the good news. She saw Dr and Mrs McKay smile with relief, and some worry lifted from their faces too.

'I see!' Mrs McKay said. 'I've been wondering what's going on. So Claire's been looking after the hedgehog babies, has she!' She smiled at her daughter. 'She loves looking after animals of any kind, you know!'

Mandy smiled too. Now she began to regret having to tell them that they might have to take Rosa's babies away from Claire for their own good. She could see now just how much they might mean to Claire.

'She's been awfully unhappy since we moved from Edinburgh,' Dr McKay told Simon. 'Taking care of these baby hedgehogs could be just what she needs!'

Simon nodded. 'From what Mandy tells me, the piglets will be between four and six weeks old,' he told the McKays. 'If I can just take a look, I can advise you on what they eat, how often and so on.'

One step at a time, Mandy thought. *Let's just make sure they're still OK.*

Chairs scraped on the tiled kitchen floor as the three of them got up to follow Mandy through to the laundry-room. Mrs McKay switched on the garage light and Claire led them all

38

into the chilly building.

She headed for the far corner, beyond her father's big silver car. 'I put their basket down by the side of the freezer,' she told Mandy. 'I put newspaper in so they wouldn't get cold.' Proudly she led the way.

Mandy felt Simon stiffen as he felt the cold. 'They'll need more than newspaper!' he whispered.

Squeezing by the car one at a time, they followed Claire to her makeshift nest.

'Oh!' Mandy heard her cry out in alarm. She was crouching over the white plastic basket.

Fear shot through her. 'What's wrong?' she cried.

Claire lifted scraps of newspaper. Her face had screwed up in panic, then the tears started. 'They've all gone!' she cried. 'There are none left!'

Mandy checked; urgently, quickly. She nodded at Simon. 'It's empty!'

'They've escaped. That basket's not deep enough. They'd be able to climb out in no time!' He too checked the empty nest.

Mrs McKay stooped to comfort Claire, but Mandy could only think of the four tiny hedgehogs. They were out alone, among the dangers of the real world! Foxes, badgers, and all the man-made traps of ponds, wire fences and busy roads lay in wait! Hunger threatened. They might get separated or lost. They could be dead already!

Mandy ran to the open garage door and stared out. Dusk had fallen; it was almost pitch black.

She looked desperately into the dark night, then ran into the middle of the McKays' lawn. She strained to see, to hear anything that might help. She listened intently.

And yes, amidst the rustling leaves she could hear another sound. A tiny, odd, pathetic sound that she remembered from earlier that afternoon. Her heart skipped and her mouth went dry. There was the sound again! It was the high, piping cry of tiny, lost hedgehogs!

CHAPTER FOUR

Mandy turned and looked at Simon, her face filled with dismay.

He joined her out on the dark lawn. 'Don't worry, we'll think of something!' he said, running one hand through his short hair.

The thought came to her in a flash. 'I know!' Mandy said. 'We could try and attract them back into the garden with a dish of food!'

'Good idea! Even though they're not completely weaned, they can still tuck into a dish of cat food!' Simon said. 'And we can ask the McKays if we can borrow thick gloves and a box to put them in. We'll be a sort of search party, up and down their hedges. A hedgehog patrol!'

'You ask for the box! I'll go next door for cat food, if Eric can spare it! Maybe James will come and help too!' Mandy forced herself to act. When she was doing something, she could push away those dreadful fears about the piglets' safety. She split off from Simon and ran next door.

James answered the doorbell with a peanut butter sandwich wedged in his mouth and a glass of Coke in one hand. His brown hair was tousled as usual, and his glasses were perched on the end of his nose.

'James, we need a dish of Eric's food to catch the baby hedgehogs! Don't ask!' she said, breathless and jumbled. 'One dish will do. And you can help if you want!'

Quickly James nodded, bolted his sandwich and raced to do as Mandy asked. 'Here's a torch!' He grabbed one from the kitchen drawer.

'And here's your jacket, James!' Mrs Hunter said. She flung it on to his back as he shot past. 'What is it this time?' she asked, confused by the search for cat food, a torch, and Mandy's breathless dash into the house.

'Operation Hedgehog!' Mandy said. 'We have to rescue Rosa's babies!'

'Oh,' Mrs Hunter said, going to the front door and holding it open. 'Rosa's babies. In that case I'd better hold on to Blackie!'

They tore down the hallway, out of the door, armed with the vital dish of food and the torch. 'Yes, please! Thanks, Mum!' James yelled back up the path.

Quickly they rejoined Simon on the McKays' lawn.

'It's OK,' Simon said. 'Dr McKay says search away. Mrs McKay's keeping Claire indoors though. She's upset enough already about the baby hedgehogs going missing!'

'I'll bet she is,' Mandy muttered. She remembered Claire's stubborn determination to 'rescue' the piglets. Being fond of animals was fine, but you also had to know what you were doing!

She set the dish of cat food on the grass. 'What now?'

Simon looked up into the night sky. The wind pushed great banks of dark clouds edged with silver across the face of the full moon. 'We wait,' he said. He pulled on woollen gloves and tied a scarf round his neck. 'Over here, out of sight.' And he led James and Mandy to the deeper shadows of the beech tree, where they squatted and began to wait.

Minutes passed and nothing happened. Only the mysterious night sounds interrupted their watch. A twig snapped in undergrowth beneath the hedge. A night bird, probably an owl, spread its wings in flight. And every now and then, the high, pleading call of the little hedgehogs crying for their mother broke the silence. 'Shh!' Simon warned. Still they waited.

'At least they haven't run away completely!' Mandy whispered. They were still circling the McKays' garden, calling and calling for their mother.

'Look!' James pointed across to the dark pyramid shape of Claire's bonfire. Something came out of the shadows.

'Too big,' Simon warned, holding Mandy back.

'It's Eric!' James cried. He'd recognised his own cat. 'He's heading for the dish of food, the cheeky thing!'

'Leave him,' Simon said. 'Just lie low and wait!'

They watched as Eric circled the dish. He stepped elegantly round it, dipped his nose towards it, raised his head, considered and turned away from the food. His ears twitched. A new sound had attracted him and off he padded, silent as a shadow.

James breathed out. 'He's just been fed,' he explained. 'Anyhow, he must have spotted something more interesting!'

They nodded.

'Shouldn't we move the dish nearer to the hedge?' Mandy suggested. 'In case the hedgehogs daren't come out into the open?'

'We could do that if we knew which hedge they were in,' Simon said. 'Their run could be anywhere, in any direction.'

Mandy nodded. 'Better leave it where it is, then.'

Still the wind chased clouds across the moon and dappled the garden with darker shadows. Still little animals rustled the grass and hopped through bushes unseen. But no baby hedgehogs appeared.

Cold almost to the bone, Mandy crouched in the shadows and shivered.

'Look, another visitor!' Simon pointed out.

This time it was an even larger, stealthier shadow than James's cat. It appeared out of nowhere, a sharp outline, still as a statue on the edge of the lawn. Then it moved precisely, menacingly forward. A white flash on its chest shone in the moonlight.

'It's a fox!' Mandy breathed. 'He's beautiful!' She saw his bright eyes glint and watched as he glided forward.

Without a second's pause he lowered his head to the dish and wolfed down the food. Then he trotted on. The brush of his tail swept the undergrowth of the hedge, and he was gone. Mandy held her breath in wonder.

Simon turned to James. 'Have you got more food at your place?' he asked.

James nodded, crept forward for the empty dish and hurried home to refill it.

'Don't give up,' Simon told Mandy. 'Those little ones can smell food from a long way off!'

'Unless that fox gets to them first,' she said, shivering again.

* * *

The new dish of food attracted many other visitors, but still not the invited guests. A tiny, sharp-nosed shrew sped across the lawn, snatched one bite and ran swiftly on. A huge stray tom-cat prowled down the drive, padding heavily towards the free meal on the grass. This time Simon stood up, jumped forward and waved his arms wildly.

He managed to scare off the old tom. 'All we need now is a badger!' he sighed as he settled back down.

'Shh!' Mandy's ears were tuned to every feeble baby hedgehog squeak. This one had sounded louder, nearer. And sure enough, a tiny round shape had stumbled out into the open. It stopped, gave a tiny snort and headed for the food dish! Mandy nearly cried out with relief.

'Wait!' Simon said steadily. 'Let him feed. The others might follow!'

Every bit of Mandy's body wanted to rush forward and rescue the piglet. But no; she waited, ready to move.

Bravely the hedgehog trotted up to

47

the food. He put his two little front paws up against the side of the dish. He nosed the mashed meat this way and that, gave one final snort and began snuffling deep into the food!

'Let's call that one Scout!' Mandy suggested. After all he was the one who had boldly gone ahead and found the trail. And to her delight, another piglet emerged from the hedge; sniffing, zigzagging, following the leader. Soon he was snorting happily, his nose deep in the dish, his stumpy tail in the air.

'That's Spike!' James said.

Then came number three. Smallest of all so far, only seven or eight centimetres long, stretching to reach the dish, stumbling head first from the rim into the food and trudging happily into the very middle, up to her ears in it. 'Tiggy!' Mandy said. She looked up, bright-eyed with excitement, at the others.

'Where's the fourth one?' James whispered, staring deep into the darkest shadows of the hedge.

Mandy heard one last, forlorn piping noise. 'Here!' she said.

The last baby came forward, looking lost and lonely. But he'd heard the snorts and he'd smelt the tempting smell. With incredible speed he darted for the dish and joined the other three in hedgehog bliss.

'And that's Speedy!' James said with a grin.

'Ready?' Simon asked.

Mandy, James and Simon put on their leather gloves and crawled forward. They prayed that the little hedgehogs would be too busy feeding to notice them. They reached the spot. All four guzzled happily on.

'Now!' Simon said with a firm nod.

Mandy moved quick as a flash to scoop up Spike in her gloved hand. His face was covered in meat and he squealed in protest as she lifted him. She noticed a small patch of broken spines behind his left ear; this was how she would remember him. Swiftly she popped him into the box Simon had brought from the house.

James too had whisked a baby to safety. It was Scout, the one with the brave zigzag movements of the explorer and the careless, untidy air. Then Simon rescued tiny Tiggy and put her, protesting, into the box with the others.

'Watch out for Speedy!' Mandy cried. For the fastest baby was making a quick getaway. The squeals of the rest had alarmed him; he was dashing for freedom again!

But Mandy half crawled, half ran across the lawn after him. In a sort of rugby tackle she managed to stop him just as he re-entered the run along the hedge. It was a rough capture, and Speedy squealed louder than the rest. But she had him safe and sound!

Mandy went back and popped the last piglet into the box.

James and Simon were grinning and slapping each other on the back. Simon gave Mandy a quick hug. 'Straight back to Animal Ark?' he asked.

She nodded. 'You'll come too, won't you?' she asked James.

'Try and stop me!' he grinned.

Together they knocked on the McKays' door to report their success.

Then on to James's house with the news, before they all piled into Simon's van, tired but thrilled.

Simon flicked on the headlights as the engine coughed into life. 'See!' He pointed to two fully-grown hedgehogs trudging down the lane ahead of them. He shook his head and waited patiently for them to sidle off into the grassy bank. 'No wonder so many get killed!'

In a minute or two the road was clear. Then they were on their way through Welford, past the busy Fox and Goose, out again along the dark road leading to Animal Ark. Simon's van, rattly and uncomfortable, got them safely home at last.

Mandy saw her mother open the door at the sound of the van. She climbed out, carrying her precious refugees, and headed down the path towards Mrs Hope.

Mrs Hope welcomed them with a broad, warm smile. 'Come in all of you, close the door!' she said. 'Let's see what you've been up to this time!' She'd changed into trousers and a big, warm sweater, ready to relax after another busy day.

Mandy grinned back at her. She put the box on the scrubbed kitchen table, feeling the warmth of the stove. They were safe! Carefully she opened the lid.

Her mother peered in and murmured, 'Oh, well done!' She beckoned them all straight through to the surgery at the back of the house. The light was on. Mr Hope was in there checking Rosa's temperature. He hummed tunelessly as he worked. He looked up at Mandy with her cardboard box.

'She's fine,' he reported. 'Her leg's already on the mend. I should be able to put on the plaster dressing soon, when the swelling's gone down.' He stared curiously at the box. 'If I'm not mistaken, you're about to make this injured hedgehog's day!' he said.

Mandy nodded and came forward. 'We found the babies! All four of them!' She beamed up at him, showing him the four young ones curled up in the bottom of the box.

'This is Scout!' she said as she picked him up, skilful now in handling the hedgehogs. She put him gingerly in the warm incubator along with his mother. 'And this little one is Tiggy. This one's Speedy, and this is Spike!' Soon all four were in the clear cage with their mother.

'Now, let's see if she'll take to them again,' Mr Hope said. 'We might be lucky!'

Mandy peered anxiously into the incubator. The babies had been handled a lot since Rosa had made her own dash for freedom. Would she be happy to see them, or would she turn against them? Mandy held her breath.

At first Rosa squeaked with surprise. Then she poked and licked and snuffled at each one in turn. She made little sideways moves, her clumsy stiff leg getting in everyone's way. Then she snorted with pleasure and shooed all her babies into one corner. They squeaked, struggled for position and grew breathless with excitement. She settled them down, bossing them with her snout.

Mandy looked up at the others in the surgery—Simon, James, her mother and father. She grinned. 'Back where they belong!' she said with a sigh.

She glanced down again, and there were four contented babies suckling, and one very happy mother hedgehog.

CHAPTER FIVE

'Animal Ark is really living up to its name!' Mrs Hope said early next morning. She watched as Mandy spooned out a dishful of fresh cat food for Rosa and her babies.

'I know, isn't it great!' Mandy agreed. Nothing felt better than rescuing animals and making sure they were safe and healthy. She placed the metal dish down in the hedgehogs' new home and watched them all tuck in.

'They've certainly got healthy appetites!' Mrs Hope laughed. 'Oops!' She watched as Rosa caught the smallest baby with her stiff leg and knocked her sideways into a bed of newspaper.

'Poor Tiggy!' Mandy laughed and set her back on her feet. 'She's a bit accident-prone!'

Mrs Hope leaned over Mandy's shoulder to watch the hedgehog antics. 'And when will it be safe to put them back into the wild?' she asked.

Mandy caught her bottom lip between her teeth. 'I don't know yet.' She'd thought of that question once, between leaping out of bed and brushing her teeth, but she'd pushed it to one side. 'We've only just rescued them,' she said. 'It's too soon to think about letting them go!'

'Yes, but you have to think about how to release them as soon as they're ready,' Mrs Hope insisted. 'All wild animals need to be set free. You know that!'

Mandy swallowed hard and nodded. 'I know.' It still wasn't something she wanted to talk about. She put down a dish of water and watched Rosa happily start to drink.

'Talk to Simon,' her mother said gently but firmly. 'He's the hedgehog expert!' And she went off to start surgery.

Mandy had ten minutes before she left for school. Ten minutes to do some very hard thinking! She gazed down at the baby hedgehogs. Already she loved this little hedgehog family. She knew each one by name and nature: brave Scout, the explorer; clumsy Tiggy; Speedy the sprinter; and Spike with the spines missing! She thought of Rosa the mother, and the nightmare of losing her babies. How could she, Mandy, bear to part with them?

Yet she recalled Claire McKay standing by her bonfire in the gloom, clutching the white basket of lost babies. 'They're mine!' Claire had shouted, sulky and mean. And in saying that, she'd almost ruined four little lives!

Of course, Claire had been upset when the babies vanished. Mandy remembered Mrs McKay rushing to comfort her. She'd cried as if the whole world had collapsed. But it had been wrong to put herself first and not think about the hedgehogs' welfare. Animals always came first with Mandy!

'I'm the same as Claire,' she told herself. 'If I say I want to keep Rosa and her babies, I'm just the same as Claire!'

So when Simon arrived to begin his day's work, Mandy had made up her mind. 'How long will it take us to get these hedgehogs fit and ready to go back?' she asked quietly. It seemed the hardest thing she'd ever said.

Simon gave her a quick, kind look. 'Back where they belong? A few days, a week at the most,' he said. 'I should say they're about five weeks old. At six they're generally ready to leave the nest and go their own way. Once their weight is up, we have to let them go straight away!'

Mandy nodded. A few days! That was hardly any time at all! 'And what do we have to do to help?'

'Feed them up. Weigh them every day. Once we get their weight up above four hundred grams or so, and once they're weaned from their mother's milk, they're ready to go!' Simon put on his white coat and buttoned it up. 'Shouldn't you be at school?' he asked.

'I'm on my way!' Mandy grabbed her schoolbag and zipped up her jacket. 'In fact, I'm out of here!'

She was on her bike, up the lane and cycling like mad to meet James at McFarlane's post office. She didn't feel like talking as they rode over the moor to school. Sometimes caring for animals was hard and it hurt!

She plunged into her school day as if maths was the most interesting subject on earth. It wasn't, but it kept her mind off Rosa and her babies. Today she needed to leave Animal Ark behind and think of other things.

*   *   *

'Part of the problem,' Simon said that evening as he took Scout out of the cage for weighing, 'is the place they've chosen for their run.'

He put the hedgehog carefully on to the dish of some ordinary kitchen scales, but Scout snorted and scrambled straight out again. Simon scratched his head.

'You mean they're too close to the

road?' Mandy asked. She scooped Scout up off the table and gave him back to Simon, who nodded. 'Once they've made a proper run, a track to follow, they stick to it?'

'Yes, because they build their nests along the route. It can be a couple of kilometres long, mind you.' Simon was developing another plan to weigh Scout. He took out a different sort of scale which worked on a spring balance, like a seesaw with hooks attached. 'Don't worry!' He grinned at Mandy as he saw her looking with alarm at the hooks. He began to make a sling from some fine white cotton fabric, and hung it from one hook.

'Two kilometres!' Mandy gasped. 'I thought they just stayed around one garden!'

'No way. Hedgehogs are travellers.' Simon placed Scout carefully in the sling and began to balance the scale with weights. He concentrated hard. 'But Rosa's run is dangerous because it seems to cross the road just outside the Hunters' place. Three hundred and ten grams!' he announced cheerfully and noted it down.

Mandy held back a groan. Scout was a fat little hedgehog, doing really well on his new luxury diet of cat food.

'Do you think you can do this?' Simon asked.

She nodded and took over. Very carefully she measured and recorded the weights of the three other piglets. None was as heavy as Scout, but all weighed in at around the three-hundred-gram mark, even Tiggy. 'What happens if they're too light?' Mandy asked.

'They won't be big enough to hibernate. Not enough body fat to carry them through the winter. Not to put too fine a point on it, they'd starve to death!' Simon had moved on to check a sickly white cockatoo with a bright yellow crest. It was new to Animal Ark and squawked moodily at Simon as he approached its cage.

'How come you know so much about hedgehogs?' Mandy asked, to change the subject. She still felt upset about letting go of Rosa and family so soon after she'd found them.

'I just like them,' he said. 'And I've a friend who did a special study on them. We were at college together. Now she works for radio, on the wildlife programme, *Wildlife Ways*. You know?' Simon chatted on. 'You'd be amazed by how much I don't know about them!' he insisted. 'Now Michelle; she's the real expert!'

They were interrupted in their work by a quick visit from James and Susan Collins. Susan was looking happier since she'd finally settled into the village. Prince, her pony, was fine too. Susan was in riding gear and looking radiant. 'Hi, Mandy! James says you just rescued some gorgeous little hedgehogs!' she said. 'Can I see them?'

Mandy left Susan cooing over them. She wanted to talk seriously to James. 'I'm wondering if we can reroute this hedgehog run,' she said. 'We don't want to put Rosa back in your garden and have her run straight out into the road again!'

James nodded thoughtfully. 'I'll think about it,' he said. 'But I don't know there's much we can do, short of digging a tunnel!'

Even Mandy agreed that was a bit too much to ask. She watched James and Susan leave together. As they crossed the surgery yard, they said hello to another familiar figure. Claire McKay had stepped out of her father's silver car and was heading straight for reception! Mandy's eyes widened. What did she want?

'Nearly home time,' Simon said. He glanced at his watch, then up at Mandy. 'Uh-oh, what's up now?'

Mandy's face had set into a frown and she pointed out of the window.

'Calm down,' Simon said. 'Let's see what she wants first.'

Claire came into reception alone. Mandy peered out curiously, then ducked back. Claire was carrying a blue shoe box with breathing holes poked into the lid. From inside the treatment room, Mandy heard her explaining to Jean. Jean murmured back. There was a pause, then Claire and the box were both shown in. 'Casualty!' Jean reported. She pointed at the shoe box, then she closed the door.

Claire hung back, her head bowed. Two straight curtains of dark hair slid forward to hide her face. Mandy suddenly thought she looked unhappy and very small.

'What have you got there?' Simon asked.

'Hedgehog,' Claire said in a faint voice. She shuffled forward and looked up at Mandy. 'I'm awfully sorry about the babies!' she said, her dark eyes full of tears. 'I never meant to harm them!'

Mandy saw how upset she was. 'You really care about them, don't you?'

Claire nodded. The tears brimmed over and began to trickle down her cheeks. 'I didn't mean to steal them!' she said.

And Mandy softened straight away. She could never hold a grudge against someone who loved animals. She went up to Claire smiling kindly. 'Never mind, they're all fine now! Is there something wrong with this one too?'

Claire nodded and opened the box without speaking. Mandy looked in on a well padded nest, warm and safe this time, with a full-sized hedgehog snuffling quietly in one corner. His back legs were all tangled in strong green plastic netting, the sort used by gardeners for supporting peas and beans. It seemed this old hedgehog had blundered into a heap of the stuff and managed to wrap it round his legs. Now he couldn't move.

'Where did you find him?' Mandy beckoned Simon across for a closer look. 'In the bottom of my bonfire,' Claire said. 'It's a good place for them, isn't it?'

Mandy nodded. 'Until we set it alight!' she warned.

'It's OK, I'll check it every day,' Claire promised. 'I've called him Guy!'

Mandy smiled, but Simon was snipping carefully at the tangled netting and looking slightly worried. 'What is it?' she asked.

'I'm not sure,' he said, freeing Guy and picking him up.

Mandy stood by Claire and waited for him to give his verdict. Claire began to tense up. 'He's OK, isn't he?' she said. 'His legs are OK now!'

'His legs are fine,' Simon said,

setting the hedgehog down. 'But his eyes aren't, I'm afraid. Take a look!'

They watched as Guy turned in tight, slow circles on the table. Simon placed a pile of paper towels in his way and the hedgehog blundered into it.

'He's blind!' Mandy said slowly.

Simon nodded. 'Probably caused by an accident.'

Mandy looked closely and saw that the normally bright, beady hedgehog eyes were dull and blank. She heard Claire begin to sniff noisily again. 'Wait!' Mandy said. She went off for a dish of fresh food and put it down on the table, some way off from Guy. 'Watch this!'

Up went his nose. He snuffled the air, scented the food and headed straight for it, true as an arrow.

'Nothing wrong with his sense of smell!' Simon agreed. 'Maybe, just maybe . . .' He put a hand to his chin, deep in thought.

Mandy guessed what was coming next. 'Are you thinking what I'm thinking?' she said. 'He's blind but not helpless?'

'That's right. Hedgehogs rely on smell more than sight anyway. There's no reason he can't have a perfectly happy life as he is. As long as—'

'As long as someone looks after him!' Mandy leapt in. Her face was full of excitement. 'He needs someone special to look after him, to put out food for him and so on!' Both she and Simon stared at Claire.

'Me!' Claire gasped. 'Me! I'll look after Guy!' She dried her eyes. 'He can live in my garden, and I won't bother him, ever! I'll just put out his food and I'll keep an eye on him. That's right, isn't it?'

Mandy grinned. 'That's exactly right!'

'Oh!' Claire smiled and her face lit up. 'I can look after him! Wait while I tell my dad!' she cried. And she dashed out to fetch him.

Simon grinned at Mandy. 'That seems to have worked out fine,' he said.

Dr McKay came back looking puzzled but interested. Mandy explained carefully.

'Sounds like a good idea,' the doctor agreed. 'And just what Claire and Guy both need!' He thanked Mandy and Simon very much.

Simon described the shape and size of nest-box which might be useful for Guy to hibernate in. 'His blindness might prevent him from collecting materials for a nest of his own,' he explained.

Mandy took Claire off to show her how well Rosa and her family were doing after just one day at Animal Ark. Claire nodded and listened as Mandy explained the type of food Guy would like.

'He'll probably still forage for slugs and things. But the food you give him will help make up for what he can't catch; the things that move more quickly, like insects and millipedes.'

Claire nodded. 'OK. He'll have loads of room in my garden. I'll look after him,' she promised.

'Loads of room!' Mandy repeated. She recalled Claire's large garden and all the hedges and bushes and shady corners that hedgehogs liked. 'Yes, it's a good place for hedgehogs,' she said thoughtfully. Then an idea struck her. 'Listen!' She darted over to interrupt Simon and Dr McKay.

Simon glanced up. 'Hang on, Mandy's just had an idea, I can tell by her face!' he warned.

'I have! And it's brilliant!' she said. She could hardly keep still for excitement. She grinned at Claire.

'Well?' Dr McKay put his head to one side, smiling.

'Well, you have a huge garden . . .'

'Ye-es!'

'And Claire loves hedgehogs . . .'

'Aye!'

'And at the end of this week we have to put Rosa and Spike and Tiggy and Scout and Speedy back into their natural habitat!'

'Aye!' Dr McKay's voice rose higher and higher.

'And your huge garden is close to their run, so they would be able to find their way around right away!' Mandy said.

'If?' Dr McKay said cautiously.

'If you let us set up a hedgehog refuge in your garden!' Mandy said.

This was her brilliant idea. 'A sort of halfway house for Rosa and her family!' Mandy raced on. She was already thinking of special cages, fenced in areas, feeding stations, lookout points. 'Please say yes!' she said. 'Just to help them get used to roaming free again!'

Dr McKay's eyebrows knitted then lifted. 'Like a hostel for hedgehogs?' He began to nod and smile.

Claire was holding tight to his hand. 'Please, Daddy!' she cried.

Mandy knew how much this would mean to Claire as well as to her. Together they'd work on the problems of putting the baby hedgehogs back into the wild.

She stared into the doctor's eyes. 'We'll call it Rosa's Refuge!' she cried. She looked down at Rosa and her gorgeous family. 'Let's all work together to set them free!'

CHAPTER SIX

'You realise we've got less than a week to set up this refuge!' Mandy told James. 'Simon says we have to let them go as soon as they're ready, so they can hibernate through the winter. The nights are already turning frosty!'

They'd just called in at McFarlane's to beg old, unsold newspapers to line hedgehog boxes. James was as keen as Mandy to get things organised. 'I'm just sorry it can't be in my garden,' he told Mandy.

Mandy slowed down and pulled her bike into the side of the road. Suddenly she saw that they'd chosen Claire's garden without talking to James.

He must be feeling left out. 'It's true, we couldn't have the hedgehogs at your place because of Blackie.'

James shrugged. 'I know.' His hair was damp from the drizzle. He seemed to be making an effort to cheer up though. 'Anyway, my dad and I have put extra wire netting along the hedge

70

so Rosa and the rest can't just wander through. Blackie won't be able to bother them again!'

Mandy protested, 'It wasn't Blackie's fault!'

'And I'm racking my brains to see what else I can do!' James went on eagerly. He set off on his bike with a determined look. 'Come on,' he said. 'I thought you wanted to get to Ernie's place before tea!'

They rode quickly on and soon arrived at Ernie Bell's place. Mandy knew Ernie was the best carpenter in the area, even though he was retired. He'd built the fence for Lydia's goats up at High Cross, and he'd built it brilliantly. Now they were going to ask Ernie another favour.

'I made a quick drawing of an idea I had for a hedgehog's nest-box,' James said once they were inside Ernie's cottage. He took a piece of paper from his pocket and spread it flat on the kitchen table.

Mandy nodded. 'It's great, Ernie!' James was brilliant at measuring and drawing.

'We both think it should work OK,' James told Ernie. 'Look, it has to have a tunnel opening with a door you can lift . . .'

'The little tunnel entrance is to keep out badgers, see!' Mandy explained. 'The hedgehogs could even hibernate in here if you put a ventilation pipe in the top!' She pointed out various places on James's drawing.

'Steady on!' Ernie laughed and took his glasses out of his shirt pocket. He studied the paper. 'It's all measured in millimetres!' he said in disgust. 'Talk to me in inches and I might be able to manage it for you!'

'Does that mean yes?' Mandy asked. 'James says his dad has got spare wood in his garage and we'd be able to use that for the nest-boxes. We'll need five or six of them,' she said rapidly.

'Five or six!' Ernie stood back, hands on hips. He breathed out noisily. 'And I expect you want them all finished yesterday!' he grumbled.

'By the end of the week,' James said, his eyes hopeful.

Behind her back, Mandy had all her

fingers crossed. 'Of course, if you can't manage it, we'd understand!'

Ernie made a noise midway between a laugh and a cough. 'Nay, you've caught me out that way before!'

'Ernie!' Mandy pretended to be shocked. 'I've never caught you out!' But she knew that if she suggested one thing, Ernic was bound to do the opposite. It was the way he was. 'But really, I mean it; if it's too much trouble . . .' She picked up James's nest-box plan and began to fold it.

'Give it here!' Ernie said with a grin. He studied the drawing again. 'No problem,' he said. 'You can have six by the end of the week.' He pocketed the plan and tapped it to make sure it was safe.

Mandy gave a little hop of pleasure. 'Thanks, Ernie!' She turned to James. 'Come on, no time to be hanging about here! There's loads to do!'

James grinned. He insisted on looking in on Sammy, Ernie's tame squirrel, and on Tiddles the cat, curled up on the flowery sofa in Ernie's sitting-room. Then they said goodbye.

'And what's the name of this hedgehog hostel?' Ernie wanted to know. He stood in his shirtsleeves at the gate.

'Rosa's Refuge!' Mandy told him.

Ernie gave a satisfied grunt and turned, ready to start work right away.

'Great!' James said as they rode off. 'I'm glad we live in Welford!' They set off back to his house to meet up with Claire. 'With people like Ernie around, we can really get things done!'

'And I'm glad you're looking more cheerful,' Mandy told him. Ernie had approved of James's plans. Now, like Claire, he was really part of Rosa's Refuge.

As they cycled out of the village, the light began to fade and an orange tinge had come into the sky. The hedgerows darkened to silhouettes. James snatched the time to tell Mandy his next idea. 'You know the problem you mentioned about the road? I've been thinking about it,' he said.

Mandy nodded. She loved the peace of these lanes, the feeling that small things went quietly about their business in the deep ditches and hedgerows while humans dashed madly by.

'Obviously we can't really dig a tunnel under the road for the hedgehogs,' James said. 'And I don't think we could train them to use a bridge! They'll have to keep on using the road as far as I can see. So what we have to do is make the cars slow down!'

'How?' She could tell when James had got stuck into an idea. His face went into a frown and he began to rush his words together.

'We make a sign!' James said. "Hedgehogs Crossing!" You know, like a "Children Crossing!" sign. It can be cows, ducks, anything!'

'Hedgehogs?' Mandy wondered. 'You mean a red triangle with a picture of a hedgehog?' Her eyes had lit up again. 'Do you think drivers would take any notice?'

'They would!' James insisted. 'If it were a good sign, properly painted, with a big notice underneath saying "Slow Down! Hedgehog Crossing!" Yes, it'd work!'

Mandy grinned. 'I think you're

right!' she said.

'So shall we make the sign?'

'Yes!' Mandy attacked the next hill with new energy. Specially built nest-boxes, a proper sign, everything! Nothing was too good for Rosa and her babies. 'Let's go and tell Claire!' she said. She paused on the crest of the hill then freewheeled down. Things happened fast when you got involved in rescuing animals. Life rushed you along!

*   *   *

Dr McKay arrived home from work looking tired and pale, but when he saw Claire helping Mandy and James to design the Hedgehogs Crossing sign at his own kitchen table, he drew up a chair to watch.

'Are we nearly ready for the grand opening? Is Rosa's Refuge going according to plan?' he asked.

All three of them nodded without looking up.

'And how long will these hedgehogs stay in your refuge?' Dr McKay took off his jacket and slung it around the back of the chair. 'I mean, how long before they're off on their own again?'

Mandy answered. 'Simon says it takes about three days for them to settle into their nests. Then we open up the doors and they're free to go!' Her voice trailed off at the picture of Rosa and the piglets wandering off into the night. 'We leave the boxes there though, in case they want to come back.'

'They will come back, won't they?' Claire asked in a worried voice.

'Oh, yes!' Mandy said. But she sounded more confident than she felt.

'Good!' Claire concentrated on her hedgehog drawing again. 'I wouldn't want them never to come back!' she said.

Dr McKay considered things as they worked and talked. 'So you'll need feeding stations? Places where you can leave food out without it being snaffled by any cheeky young cat, for instance?' He raised an eyebrow at James. He'd obviously heard of Eric's reputation. 'Don't worry about the cost of the food, by the way. I'll give you some money to cover that.'

'Thanks, Dr McKay!' James said. He grinned at Claire and Mandy.

'My idea is to put the dish of food at the centre of a loose coil of wire mesh. You fit a lid over the top. It's like a maze; you have to follow the path into the centre.' He drew them a quick pencil sketch. 'It's too small for cats, but wee hedgehogs have a knack of squeezing through narrow places, eh?' He paused to see what they thought.

'Brilliant!' Mandy said.

'Aye, well, I've been thinking of making such a thing for Guy in any case.' He smiled at his daughter. 'So maybe I'll just make a few more!'

Claire beamed up at her father. 'Do you like my drawing?' she asked. It was a big, bold black and white drawing of a hedgehog, all prickles, snout and feet. James was designing a red triangle, and the words, 'Slow Down! Hedgehogs Crossing!' to fit underneath.

Dr McKay gave her a cuddle. 'Terrific!' he said.

'I think we'll be ready!' Mandy said.

'I can hardly believe it!' Each hour seemed to bring them closer to making life safer for Rosa and her babies.

But out at the gate, just where Rosa had had her accident, Mandy had another shaky reminder of the important job they had to do.

It was already dark, and Mr Hope had arrived to take Mandy home. She said goodbye to the others and put her bike into the back of the Landrover. Then she climbed in. She was tired but pleased. They'd all worked hard on Rosa's Refuge and her father gave her a sympathetic grin. He switched on the headlights. Mandy waved at James and Claire then she faced forward, sinking deep into the comfortable seat.

Suddenly she shot forward. 'Oh, no!' She unclipped her seat-belt. 'Oh, Dad, look!'

There on the road, ten metres ahead, creeping along at snail's pace, snuffling and poking into the muddy puddles, was yet another young hedgehog! Mandy slipped quickly out of her seat, down on to the grass verge.

'Mind the road!' Mr Hope warned.

He followed quickly.

Mandy went ahead. She saw clearly how so many hedgehogs managed to get themselves run over. This one didn't scuttle off sideways into the long grass at the blinding glare of lights. No, this hedgehog had simply stopped dead still and curled up in the very middle of the road! He was a sitting target!

'That's exactly the wrong thing to do!' Mandy told him. But how was he to know? She looked and listened for traffic. No cars were coming, thank heavens. 'Lend me your jacket, Dad,' she said urgently.

Mr Hope glanced down at his best leather jacket. He looked from it down at the hedgehog curled up still as a statue in the road. 'Oh no!' he said, putting two and two together. He made as if to zip up his jacket tight.

But Mandy insisted. 'Yours is good thick leather! Take it off quickly, Dad, please! There might be a car coming!'

She didn't have any gloves to protect her hands, so she waited while her father took off his jacket. Then she took it and wrapped it round her hands. Gently she rolled the hedgehog on to it. Once it was safely cradled in the leather jacket, she walked back towards James and Claire. 'We'll put it in the garden with a dish of food,' she said. 'Then it'll be safe.'

'Lucky it was you setting off down the road,' James said. He gave a hand with the food and soon the hedgehog was tucking happily into the free meal. 'One more hedgehog saved!'he added.

'One more accident waiting to happen!' Mandy sighed. 'I only hope your crossing sign works!'

At last they could set off home. Mandy was doing all she could, but life for the hedgehogs was still full of dangers.

Mandy was deep in thought as Mr Hope drove home. Tomorrow was the big day. Ernie's nestboxes would be ready for collection, and James and Claire's sign could be put up by the road. Scout, Speedy, Tiggy and Spike were gaining twenty or thirty grams in weight each day. Rosa's leg was in plaster now, but she'd got so used to it that she could move on three legs almost as fast as Speedy on four! Nothing could get in the way. Rosa's Refuge was about to open!

She should feel happy and excited, she told herself. A hedgehog hostel was a great thing to be setting up. But she thought of Claire having to say goodbye to the babies if they decided to go off to new gardens, or new fields and hedgerows. Poor Claire had had so many goodbyes already this year, to her old house and her friends in Scotland. But perhaps tomorrow would be different, she told herself. Perhaps tomorrow, when it all actually happened, they would be glad!

*   *   *

'Don't you ever go home?' Mr Hope asked Simon. He was putting instruments into the sterilising unit.

It was teatime of the big day. Simon was giving Scout and the other young hedgehogs one last check over. 'Once in a while I do manage to call in there,' he grinned. He gave Mandy the figure for Scout's weight chart. 'Four hundred and five grams!' he announced.

Mandy wrote it down and sighed. 'They're ready!' she said.

'They are,' Simon agreed.

'Tonight's the night!' Mr Hope said.

'Tonight's the night!' the sick white cockatoo mimicked. He wagged his head sideways and danced on his perch.

'You're feeling better!' Mr Hope commented.

They all laughed. Mandy helped to lift Rosa and her family in their special cage into the back of Simon's van. She'd arranged to meet James and Claire at Rosa's Refuge at six. Dusk was already falling. It was a misty, still evening. Damp leaves squelched underfoot. 'It's all right, calm down,' Mandy whispered to Rosa. The hedgehog had raised her head to sniff at the old familiar garden smells from the safety of her cage. 'No need to worry. We're taking you home!'

Mandy's voice seemed to calm her and she settled back amidst the prickly heap of sleeping bodies.

'We have to call at Ernie's on the

way, remember!' she said to Simon.

He nodded and started up the engine as Mandy climbed in.

'Good luck!' Mr Hope said, leaning against Mandy's open window. He gave her one of his lopsided grins.

'Thanks, Dad!'

She kept one wary eye on their passengers all the way down the bumpy road. She wished Simon's van wasn't quite so old and rattly. Outside the Fox and Goose, Simon pulled in. Mandy hopped out, down the side of the pub to the row of cottages where Ernie lived.

'Hello, Walter!' Mandy called out and waved to Walter Pickard, a neighbour of Ernie's who had a house full of cats. He waved back through the cosy square of lighted window.

Ernie was at his own door, waiting to greet her. 'I was beginning to think you'd got lost!' he grumbled.

'I said half past five!' Mandy protested.

'Aye, and it's twenty-five to six!' Ernie pointed out. He handed her a nest-box. 'Well, what's the verdict?' he asked.

Mandy looked at the beautifully made box, the size of a portable television, with a little tunnel entrance jutting out of the front and a piece of ventilator pipe sticking up from the roof. 'It's wonderful!' she said. 'It's absolutely wonderful!'

She and Simon helped him carry all six of the boxes into the van. No hedgehog could wish for better accommodation!

'And!' said Ernie on the last trip back to his cottage. 'I've made you a little something else!' He stood on his doorstep, hands in pockets, grinning.

'What is it?' Mandy asked.

Ernie leaned back behind the door and drew out a wooden board cut into the shape of a house. It was a sign of some sort, with two short chains to hang it up. Ernie swung it in front of Mandy. Letters were etched into the wooden surface and stained dark brown. The board shone with clear varnish: 'Rosa's Refuge' the letters read, big and bold. Underneath was a row of five stars!

Mandy laughed. 'A five star hotel for hedgehogs!' she said with delight, and took the sign from Ernie. 'We'll hang it from a tree in Claire's garden!' she promised. 'So everyone will know!'

She felt very proud as they drove off, and her spirits soared.

In any case, when they arrived at Claire's house with the nest-boxes, the sign and the hedgehogs themselves, Mandy discovered there was no chance of keeping quiet about Rosa's Refuge.

'Who are all these people?' she asked Simon. She recognised Dr and Mrs McKay, Mr and Mrs Hunter, James and Claire. But in amongst the group were people she'd never seen before. One of them carried a camera over his shoulder.

'Ah, it's a surprise,' Simon said, studying his fingernails and pretending to look embarrassed. 'These are just some people I phoned and invited along to the grand opening!'

And that was all he had time to say before everyone came running up. 'Where are the hedgehogs?' someone asked. There was a buzz of excitement in the air.

'Could we have a picture of Mandy, James and Claire?' said the man with the camera.

'They're reporters!' James whispered, his face red and shiny. 'They heard about Rosa's Refuge. They want to put it in the local paper!'

'Oh, no!' Mandy gasped. She was hustled into the garden.

Ernie's shiny sign was hung from the beech tree. Then James and Claire had to hold up their own red triangle sign. 'A bit closer, that's right! Hold the sign up a bit, that's good! Now smile!' the photographer called as they stood in line. They smiled and the camera flashed. 'Great, thanks!' he said.

'Blame me,' Simon said to Mandy. 'I thought you deserved to have your names in the paper for this!'

Mandy had gone red from smiling into the camera, but the photographer gave way to another stranger. He asked lots of questions about how they'd rescued Rosa after her accident, and how they'd helped her look after her babies. Mandy explained the idea of Rosa's Refuge. 'It'll be their pre-release place to stay, nice and safe, until they feel happy to explore and make their own nests again,' she said.

The fair-haired reporter began to write down her answers. 'Ready for winter?' he asked.

Mandy nodded. 'Yes, now's the time when they hibernate. We want them to lead normal hedgehog lives. They need every chance we can give them,' she said.

'And that's the idea of the "Hedgehogs Crossing" sign too?' The reporter sounded really interested. He was writing everything down.

Mandy nodded again. 'Can you put that in the paper, please? This road is a busy hedgehog run. We want cars to slow down and give way!' She tried to make sure that he told his readers that. 'It was James Hunter's idea! And Rosa's Refuge was thought up by Claire McKay and me! This is Claire's garden. We couldn't have done it without her!'

He wrote it down. 'Good! And now just one last question,' he said, pencil poised.

'Yes?' Mandy was keen now to get on with the real job of setting up the nest-boxes in good, secret corners of Claire's garden.

'Well, you've gone to all this trouble to save the hedgehogs' lives. Our readers will really admire you for that. But how will you know if it's worked? How will you know whether or not they've survived?'

Mandy let the question gradually sink in. 'We won't,' she said faintly.

He clicked his tongue. 'Pity,' he said. 'That would have made a perfect happy ending to the story!' Then he shut his notebook, thanked her very much and went off to collect his photographer. 'Look in next week's paper!' he called. They stood by their car, ready to leave. Then waving cheerfully, they drove off.

And then everyone had to lend a hand to get the nest-boxes into place. They chose shady places and disguised each one with twigs and leaves. Then they set up the doctor's wire mesh feeding stations. It was a busy, bustling

89

time. Claire chose a special place for Guy's nest-box, close to the garden shed where she could keep an eye on him. Mandy made sure that all the tunnel entrances to the nest-boxes were clear.

It was all helped along by cups of tea from Mrs McKay. The lawn was criss-crossed by torchlight beams, wellington boots, voices calling. At last it was time to fetch Rosa, Scout, Spike, Tiggy and Speedy from the van. Mandy lifted their cage with great care and carried them over.

They held their breath as Mandy put on a pair of sturdy garden gloves and peered down into the cage. She chose Spike and picked him up first. 'Today's Friday!' she told him. 'If you stay in your new box for three days, on Monday we'll open your door and you'll be free to go!'

He grunted. Free to roam the hedgehog runs in gardens and fields, Mandy thought. Through hedges and into woodlands. He would be a wild hedgehog again!

Spike sniffed her glove and waggled

his fat little body from side to side.

Mandy smiled fondly down, but she couldn't get Claire's worried look and the reporter's final question out of her mind! 'How will you know if they've survived?' he'd asked. And her own answer: 'We won't!'

She felt Claire smiling bravely at her. There was a catch in her own throat as she crouched down close to the ground with Spike. Mandy showed him the cosy box Ernie had made. 'We won't know,' she told herself. 'We won't ever know!'

CHAPTER SEVEN

Spike, Speedy, Tiggy, Scout and Rosa all moved without a hitch into their special nest-boxes in Rosa's Refuge. Claire was thrilled when she could bring Guy along to join them.

'You can leave his door open right away,' Simon told her. 'We know he can poke and potter around in the garden by himself. Are you feeding him up well for the winter?'

Claire nodded. She put the blind hedgehog into his smart new nest-box and sighed happily.

'Come and tell me if this is a good place for the road sign!' James called. He struggled with the large white triangle edged with red, showing Claire's drawing of a hedgehog. At last he held it, shoulder high, against a fence post outside his garden.

Mandy went and stood a few metres down the road to judge the effect. 'That's great!' she said. 'Everyone can see that clearly!'

Then they had to go and make sure that all Rosa's family had enough food and bedding inside their boxes. For a moment Mandy stooped to peer in at one of them. She watched as Tiggy, still the smallest, dived into the middle of the messy heap of leaves and newspaper. Then Tiggy began turning round and round on the spot, using her spines to comb the nest lining into place. Soon she had a neat-looking, round nest. 'So that's how it's done!' Mandy said, impressed.

They all made one final check around Rosa's Refuge. They pegged the wire feeding stations into place with tent pegs and made sure each had a dish of food and one of water for any of the local wild hedgehogs who fancied a free supper. Rosa's Refuge was to be open to all.

'Ready?' Simon asked.

Mandy looked at Claire and nodded reluctantly.

'Come on then, let's go.' Simon blew warm breath on to his cold fingers. 'See you tomorrow!' he said to James and the McKays. 'Come on, Mandy!' He stood by the van, stamping his feet.

'Don't worry,' Mandy told Claire. 'Everything's going according to plan!' She gazed around the garden. The nests were well hidden. The hedgehogs were safe inside. The 'Rosa's Refuge' sign swung slightly in the breeze. All was well.

She waved and jumped into the van without smiling. Simon drove carefully off.

'The "Hedgehogs Crossing" sign

looks good; very easy to see!' he commented. 'Let's hope it works!'

Mandy just nodded. Simon headed for Welford.

'Do you want to tell me about what's worrying you and Claire?' he asked.

Mandy looked out at the cheerful, lively scene inside the Fox and Goose. People were chatting, drinking and having a good time. Somehow, it made her feel worse. She glanced at Simon's thin, serious face. His glasses winked and shone under the street lamps. Perhaps he would understand why they still felt low.

'I know Rosa's Refuge is a great success,' she sighed, 'and everyone has worked really hard on it . . .'

'But?' Simon prompted. He signalled and turned up the lane to Mandy's house.

'But Claire and I feel the same way. We want the hedgehogs to stay in Rosa's Refuge. Otherwise we won't know what happens to them,' she confessed. 'I can stand having to let them go. But I can't stand not knowing if they're alive or dead!' Her lips trembled as she spoke.

Simon nodded. He steered up the lane to Animal Ark.

'I know; you're going to tell me that's just the way it is,' Mandy said miserably. 'There's nothing we can do to keep track of hedgehogs once they're set free!' She tucked her chin into her warm scarf and screwed up her face to fight back the tears.

But she was mistaken. 'Keep track, you say?' Simon said slowly. 'Is that what's been bothering you two?'

'Yes. Claire says she'll have nightmares about foxes and cars and badgers and . . .' She could run on endlessly through all the disasters Scout or Tiggy might meet.

'I see!' Simon said. He slowed down and stopped at the gate of Animal Ark. 'Keeping track!' he said again. He waited until Mandy had climbed out of the van and watched as she used her key to unlock the front door. Mrs Hope was hovering in the hall. 'Mandy!' he called.

'Yes?' She came running back to meet him, curious about the new tone in his voice.

'Listen, I can't promise anything!' he said quickly. 'But I've had an idea. I want you to come down to my place around lunch-time tomorrow, OK?'

'Why?' she said.

'Can't tell you yet. I'll tell you tomorrow!' he said, looking excited and secretive. And he drove off without another word.

* * *

'How did the grand opening go last night?' Mr Hope yawned over his morning newspaper.

Mandy gulped down her orange juice. 'Fine!' She was already looking at her watch. The gap between breakfast and lunch seemed endless. What was Simon's secret? She had to wait another five hours before she found out.

'Your mother tells me you're going to be famous!' her father said. His mouth twitched into a smile. 'Rosa's Refuge is going to be in the newspaper!'

96

Mandy pulled a face. 'It's all Simon's fault! He invited all those people from Walton!'

Mr Hope grinned. 'He's very proud of what you and James and Claire have done for those hedgehogs!'

Mandy felt a warm glow of pleasure. 'Hmm. They say it'll be in the paper next week. Now I have to go and check on Rosa and company!' she said, jumping up and grabbing her jacket. 'And then I'm off to Simon's flat!' As usual, she was already halfway out of the door before she'd finished speaking.

Rosa's Refuge looked calm in the crisp morning light. Mandy had called on James and Claire, and together they trudged through banks of fallen leaves to check the empty dishes in the feeding stations. Then they looked over the six nest-boxes to make sure they hadn't been disturbed. Everything seemed fine.

But Mandy felt Claire tug at her sleeve and whisper something in a worried voice. 'Mandy, you do think they'll come home, don't you?' she said again. 'I mean, Guy comes home every morning, so Rosa and her babies will too!'

'We don't know that for sure,' Mandy had to remind her gently. 'The important thing is to make it safe for them to go free again. That's why we've set up Rosa's Refuge, remember!'

'But I don't want them to go away!' Claire said in a trembling voice.

'Nobody does,' James said quietly.

Mandy looked at Claire. 'I think Simon's got an idea that might help,' she told her. She couldn't bear it when Claire looked so unhappy. 'But we have to wait until lunch-time before he tells me what it is.'

Claire looked up and nodded bravely. 'OK,' she said. She did seem suddenly happier, as if Mandy could sort out the whole world's problems.

Mandy only wished she could! She and James filled the rest of the morning by taking Blackie for a long walk into the woods behind James's house. They watched the black Labrador race through the trees after a stick. He skidded down slopes to fetch it and charged back breathless and delighted. At least it kept their minds off Simon's secret.

'Good boy, Blackie, good boy!' James said. Mandy patted his flank, glad that he'd recovered from the hedgehog attack.

'Time to go!' James decided at last. They led Blackie back home. Mandy left him with James and cycled into Walton. It was almost lunch-time! She propped her bike against the stone gatepost of Simon's house. He lived in the ground floor flat of a big old house, in a room cluttered with empty cups, old wildlife magazines and a full set of drums. She knocked on the heavy green door and waited. Simon opened it and greeted her with mock surprise. 'Mandy!' Then he broke down into a grin. 'So you didn't forget?'

'As if!' Mandy walked past him into his room. It was messy as usual, but there was a woman sitting in the single battered armchair. She stood up when Mandy went in.

'Mandy, I'd like you to meet Michelle Holmes. Remember, I told you about her? She's the real hedgehog expert!' Simon introduced them.

'You work for *Wildlife Ways*!' Mandy said, thrilled to meet Michelle. She was a small, dark woman with short dark hair and big silver earrings, dressed in practical black trousers and a thick crimson sweater. But what was she doing here, Mandy wondered. Was she part of Simon's secret?

Michelle smiled at Mandy and picked up her mug of coffee from the mantelpiece. 'Simon's been telling me about your great work at Rosa's Refuge!' she said. 'It's one of the best projects I've heard about for quite a while!'

Mandy nodded and waited. She felt there was more to come. What was Simon up to? He stood rocking his feet against the tiled fireplace, looking innocent.

'He was telling me that you want to set up a tracking system for your hedgehogs, once you release them into the wild?'

Mandy's heart jumped. 'Yes!' she cried. 'But how do you track a hedgehog through all those dark little runs? You can't even see them, let alone tell which one's which! Anyway, I don't see how you can!' she admitted.

Michelle nodded. 'It's hard. But I've been thinking about it for our programme. It's all to do with tiny radio transmitters that send out a special signal for each animal.' She sounded excited as she described her idea to Mandy. 'You fix the transmitter to your fox, or your badger or your hedgehog—whatever—with a tiny sterile pin. It's a bit like piercing the base of the ear, really. The pin has a small tag which glows in the dark. And it has a radio signal which we receive on this hand-held receiver.'

Michelle took something like a mobile phone out of a shoulder bag and placed it on Simon's table. 'The signal can be picked up from a distance of one kilometre and it gets louder as you get nearer to the transmitter—just right for your little hedgehogs' nightly rambles!'

Mandy took a deep breath. 'It's brilliant!' she said, still hardly daring to hope.

'Simon rang me last night and told me about your plans to set your hedgehogs free,' Michelle went on. 'He said you were keen to track them, and of course I said, "Look no further!"' She paused and smiled. 'Would you let me try out my transmitters on Rosa and her family for *Wildlife Ways*?' she asked.

Mandy closed her eyes. Had she heard this right? Was it true? She opened them again. 'When?' she asked breathlessly.

'When will you be ready to start?'

'Monday!' Mandy told her.

'Monday it is!' Michelle agreed.

*　　*　　*

After that Mandy sailed through the weekend. She was brimming full of excitement.

She rang James and Claire right away to tell them the good news. Claire was thrilled. 'Does that mean we can follow them wherever they go?' she asked.

'Yes, it means we won't lose them once we set them free!'

There was a pause, then Claire said, 'You're great, Mandy! You're the best friend anyone could ever have!' Then she put the phone down in a rush.

Mandy sighed happily. She thought of Claire when they'd first met; moody and pale, lonely and frightened. It was all changed now, thanks to Operation Hedgehog!

She went away and bubbled over with the news to everyone she met.

'We're going to track the hedgehogs!' she told her grandparents when they came to tea on Saturday. 'We'll be able to track exactly where they are with a radio transmitter!'

Her grandfather thought that the technology was wonderful. 'They never had anything like that in my day!' he said.

'And what a thrill to be on *Wildlife Ways*!' Gran said. 'I always listen to that!'

Mandy sat cross-legged on the sofa, totally happy.

'I wish it was Monday!' she said to

James and Claire on Sunday at teatime. They were checking the hedgehog nests at dusk as usual, and saying hello to Guy. 'We'll be able to do the tracking each dawn and dusk until we're sure everyone's OK. Will you be able to come too?'

James nodded. 'I've told my mum and dad it's a scientific experiment,' he said.

'It is!' Mandy insisted. 'And it's the first of its kind!' She felt very important, and honoured that Michelle had chosen them.

Claire followed them round, her face lit up with silent excitement. But as Mandy got ready to leave, Claire took her to a quiet spot under the beech tree. 'I don't mind at all now!' she announced bravely.

Mandy smiled. Claire sometimes said things in a funny, old-fashioned way that made her sound older than eight. 'What don't you mind?' she said.

'Having to let them go! As long as we know where they are, I'll be perfectly happy!'

'Me too.' Mandy gave her a quick

hug.

'We do have to let them go, don't we?' Claire said quickly.

'We do.' Mandy was suddenly serious. Claire was learning a lot about letting things go. They'd help each other to get over it. 'We have to start on Monday!' she said.

Claire nodded and seemed to accept what Mandy told her. Slowly she went up the steps into her house.

*　　　*　　　*

Monday teatime arrived at last. Simon had arranged to bring Michelle straight to Rosa's Refuge. They arrived just as daylight began to fade.

Mandy was there early. 'Let's choose Spike and Speedy for the first day,' she said to James. 'They're nice and strong and healthy.'

James held Speedy, ready for Michelle to arrive, and Mandy herself held Spike. Claire was with them, wrapped in a blue anorak and scarf, ready and willing to help.

Michelle strode up and put her bag

on the lawn. 'I've brought the transmitters,' she said. 'Are these the brave explorers who'll help us carry out our experiment?'

Spike blinked and snuffled. Mandy nodded. 'This is Spike.' She watched carefully as Michelle took out a thumbnail-sized metal tag with a tiny aerial attached to it.

'Great!' Michelle inspected him. 'He even has a little bald patch to which the transmitter could be attached!' She set to work, punching a tiny hole in the skin at the base of his ear to keep the tag in place.

Soon Spike was fixed up with the new tracking device. He sat quietly in Mandy's hand, snorting at the fresh air smells.

'He looks funny!' Claire giggled.

'He can hardly wait!' Simon laughed.

Michelle worked quickly to attach a second luminous tag and aerial to Speedy. Soon both hedgehogs were ready.

'Right,' Michelle said. She checked the two signals on her receiver. Spike's was a low and slow bleep, while

Speedy's was high and fast. 'That's fine. Are you ready?' she asked Mandy.

Mandy took a deep breath. 'Ready!' she said.

'We'll follow Spike first, OK?' Michelle asked.

Mandy looked down at Spike. His tag glowed bright green in the gathering dark. His signal bleeped loudly on Michelle's receiver. 'Good luck!' she whispered to him. And she set him down on the lawn.

'We've all got our fingers crossed for him,' Simon told her. 'Look, he's off!'

They listened and watched as Spike, with his little green light, snorted and darted for the nearest hedge.

'Come on!' Michelle said to Mandy. just you and me—not too much fuss!'

But James said, 'Hang on!' and whispered something to Michelle.

Michelle nodded. 'OK, Claire, you come too!'

Claire shot forward to join Mandy and Michelle.

They followed the light at a distance of about thirty metres. It zigzagged from hedge to bush, then back to hedge. It circled the beech tree at the back of Rosa's Refuge, then it darted under a fence towards the woodland where Mandy had walked Blackie on Saturday.

'I can't see him!' Mandy whispered. She'd lost him in the long grass and undergrowth.

'No, but I can hear him loud and clear!' Michelle said. She followed where the low, slow bleeps came loudest. 'Look!'

They picked up the green light again, standing stock-still in the middle of a small clearing.

'Why has he stopped?' Claire wondered. 'What's wrong?'

She hadn't finished whispering before they saw the answer. Spike had picked up a scent and rolled into a tight ball. He'd smelt danger!

Out of the low laurel bushes opposite came the menacing shape of a fox! He must have heard Spike snorting among the leaves for slugs and come to investigate!

Mandy crouched in the long grass, afraid. Would Spike know what to do when danger came? She glanced across at Claire, then fixed her gaze on Spike's little green light and prayed.

The fox dipped his head towards Spike. He sniffed. He dipped his nose towards the hedgehog, but didn't touch the spikes. He put out one front paw, as if to tap the prickly ball.

At that second, Spike unrolled and prepared to sprint.

'Oh, don't!' Claire said. 'Roll up again, quick!' The fox's jaw snapped within millimetres of Spike's back legs. Quick as a flash, Spike rolled up again, and when the fox made a second lunge, his nose met hedgehog spines, sharp and strong. He yelped, then howled, shook his head and sloped off. The clearing fell silent. Spike had won!

'A fox seldom gets the better of a hedgehog!' Michelle said, smiling. 'It's only badgers they really have to worry about! And that's only natural; badgers have to hunt and eat something, after all!'

Mandy nodded, relieved to see Spike unroll unharmed. He began to forage happily for food again. She felt pleased and proud for Spike as he set off on his first solo journey.

'I think we'll let him go off and roam on his own now,' Michelle said. 'We only have to worry about one more thing.' She paused as they watched Spike set off further afield, his green light glowing.

'What's that?' Mandy asked.

'Well, we've seen he can survive in the wild all right,' Michelle pointed out. 'But will he come back to his nest, or will he go off on his own and build new ones?'

Claire ran up to Michelle. 'You mean, will Spike come home?' she gasped. 'But won't he just come back in the morning, like Guy?'

Michelle shrugged. 'We'll have to wait and see. Come on. We'll try and pick up his signal again later if we have time! Now it's Speedy's turn!'

They turned back together through the dark woods.

Mandy and Claire looked over their shoulders every five seconds, but they'd lost sight of Spike's little green light.

'Oh!' Mandy said to herself. She felt

exactly how Claire must have felt when she had to leave Scotland. 'It's the hardest thing in the world to say goodbye!'

CHAPTER EIGHT

On that first night of freedom Speedy lived up to his name. James held him as Michelle checked his radio transmitter. Claire took a second or two to say goodbye, then James set him carefully on the lawn.

Mandy watched as the fast little hedgehog paused for just one moment. Then he raced off at top speed, straight under the shed where Claire's father kept his lawnmower!

Michelle followed, with her radio receiver going bleep bleep bleep, fast and high. She shook her head. 'We'll never fish him out from under there!'

Mandy wondered why he'd made a beeline for the shed.

'Maybe there's an old nursery nest under there too!' Michelle said. 'One that Rosa built for her babies.'

Mandy got down on all fours to see if she could spot Speedy's green light. But she could only hear the snorts and snuffles of a very happy young hedgehog. 'Plenty of slugs and worms under there!' she reported.

Claire crouched down beside her. 'Do you want to get him out?' she asked.

Mandy nodded. 'We need to track him a bit further than this to check that he can manage,' she said.

So Claire went off and came back straight away with Guy's feeding dish. She tapped it loudly with a fork. 'Here, Guy! Here, Guy!' she called.

And sure enough, grizzled old Guy came snuffling out of the hedge bottom. Claire scooped some cat food out of a tin into his dish and set it on the grass near the shed. Guy sniffed hungrily, his pointed nose in the air. Then he headed for supper.

'He always comes when I call!' Claire said proudly. 'And I bet Speedy will too!'

They waited, all eyes on the dark

shed. Soon Michelle's signal for Speedy grew stronger, and then the little green light appeared from deep under the base of the shed.

'He's coming!' Mandy whispered.

The green light edged into the open. They could just make out Speedy's tiny, domed shape. Slowly he came out and sniffed the air.

Guy raised his head from the dish and listened. He turned his blind head. Then he sidled around the dish, as if making space for a guest. Speedy watched and waited. Then, true to form, he came at racing-car speed to join Guy at supper.

Noses deep in the dish, the two new friends ate greedily.

'Well done!' Mandy whispered to Claire.

Claire beamed back at her. 'Guy will look after him!' she promised.

When the dish was empty, the old hedgehog sniffed the air. He listened and waited for Speedy, then set off steadily up the lawn towards the road, with the young hedgehog in tow. He listened again at the gate, sidling against Speedy to make him slow down too.

'Look, he's teaching him road safety!' James breathed.

Michelle smiled. 'He's just a wise old hedgehog, that's all,' she smiled.

They all watched fascinated as Guy and Speedy safely crossed the road. Michelle followed with her receiver, and she and Mandy stood by the fence opposite Rosa's Refuge watching Speedy's light criss-cross the field. 'Plenty of slugs in that long grass!' Michelle confirmed. 'And with Guy to give him good advice, I should think that Speedy's first night of freedom will be fine too!'

'Speedy can be Guy's eyes!' Mandy said. 'He can see for him. They'll look after each other!' She felt happy that the second baby was beginning to find his own way in the world. And she saw from Claire's proud smile that she was glad too.

'OK?' Michelle asked, packing away her radio gear. 'And ready for the dawn chorus? We have to be back here, ready and waiting, before daybreak!'

They all nodded. 'We'll be here!' they promised.

* * *

Mandy hardly slept at all that night. Even taking off her clothes and climbing into bed was hard to do. All her thoughts were with Spike and Speedy. When she did sleep, she dreamt of dark fields and woodlands where hedgehogs roam, and of moonless, misty nights.

She woke well before dawn. How were Spike and Speedy? Had they survived the night? Would they find their way back home? Mandy couldn't stop the questions in her head.

At first she refused breakfast, but Mrs Hope made her eat at least a scrap of toast and drink some tea. She made her wrap up well, hugged her, and wished her good luck.

Mandy liked the rough, warm feel of her mother's dressing-gown, and her dark red hair falling loose over her shoulders. 'Thanks,' she smiled.

'Is Simon coming here to collect

you?' Mrs Hope looked out of the kitchen window at the foggy early morning sky.

Mandy nodded. 'Michelle and Simon are coming here first, then we're off to track Spike and Speedy.' She sighed. 'I only hope they come back!'

Mrs Hope looked at Mandy and smiled warmly. She put an arm around her shoulder. 'Whatever happens,' she said, 'you're doing your very best for those young hedgehogs. And that's the most anyone can ask!'

Soon Simon arrived, bleary eyed and pinched by the cold. Michelle sat in the van, wrapped in a huge padded jacket with a high, zipped collar. 'Hi!' she said to Mandy.

Being a wildlife radio presenter wasn't all fun, Mandy decided. They drove off in silence between shadowy hedges, lost in the mist. The hills were invisible and, except for the milk delivery van, the village was silent and empty.

They pulled up outside James's house before dawn had fully broken. Mandy went up to his door. James was waiting in the hallway and came out to greet her, looking nervous and worried. 'Do you think they'll come back?' he asked.

Mandy shrugged. 'I don't know. Anyway, come on!'

Claire too had watched Simon's van pull up in the lane. Wrapped in her blue anorak as usual, she was waiting for them on the lawn. The Rosa's Refuge sign creaked, hardly visible in the grey light. Michelle brought her receiver from the van and they all stood in a huddle on the cold, wet grass.

'What do we do now?' Claire asked.

'Wait. What else?' Simon said.

A crow rose from a branch high in the beech tree and flapped heavily over the lawn. The trees dripped in the heavy mist.

Michelle switched frequencies on her receiver. She concentrated hard, trying to catch any faint sound; either the slow, steady bleep of Spike's signal, or the rapid, high sound of Speedy's.

'Any sign?' Simon asked. He was beginning to look concerned. It was nearly daylight. Surely Spike and Speedy should have returned by now.

Michelle shook her head. 'No, they're not back yet. Sometimes the signal can get blocked by hedgebanks, or by a high wall.' She too looked serious.

Mandy stamped her feet on the cold ground. Her breath came out in damp clouds. Waiting was too much to bear. Quietly she walked the length of the lawn, up to Claire's front gate. Claire followed silently. They peered down the misty road. 'Where are you, Spike?' Mandy breathed. 'Where are you, Speedy?'

She stared and stared, and there, almost in answer to her worried call, were two little round shapes! They were easy to mistake at first for stones or clumps of earth, but they were moving steadily towards her in the middle of the road, side by side. One had the telltale radio tag and antenna. One was old and blind.

'It's Speedy!' Claire cried. 'And Guy! They're back! Oh, Mandy, they've come home!'

Michelle and James came running up the lawn. The receiver bleeped loudly. 'I've got him!' Michelle confirmed. Then she began to speak excitedly, though quietly, into a small black tape recorder. 'The first of the hedgehogs to return to Rosa's Refuge is Speedy. The time is seven forty-five a.m. Speedy was released at ten past eight last night. His return, with a blind hedgehog, Guy, marks success for the Welford rescue team!' She pressed a button and beamed at Mandy. 'Good news!' she said.

'Look!' Mandy watched as Speedy circled once round Guy, then trotted off. He headed off down the lawn straight for his own nest-box, paused once at the little tunnel entrance, sniffed and vanished. Mandy breathed a huge sigh of relief.

'And here, right on cue, comes hedgehog number two!' Simon called. He peered over the hedge at the back of the McKays' garden.

The mist lifted as day finally broke, and Michelle's receiver was picking up Spike's low signal loud and clear. Spike trundled across the flower-beds, heading for home.

Michelle spoke again into her recorder, her voice quiet and dramatic at the same time. 'Spike, the second hedgehog, is arriving home at seven forty-nine a.m. He's in good shape and heading for his nest-box. There seems little doubt that both hedgehogs are fit and well, and easily able to survive in the wild!' She pressed the stop button. Spike was already inside his dry, warm box, even now fast asleep.

'Brilliant!' Mandy breathed. James grinned broadly. Claire ran and checked to see that Guy was safely home, then she joined them.

'Speedy came back!' she said, jumping up and down. She let out little clouds of steamy breath into the cold air. 'Guy brought him home!' She danced for joy.

'Tonight it's Tiggy and Scout's turn!' Mandy said.

'Don't worry, I don't need a reminder!' Michelle laughed. 'I'll be here!' She zipped up her shoulder bag. 'With two new transmitters and two new signals!' She turned cheerfully to Simon. 'This is great,' she said. 'Just what the listeners of *Wildlife Ways* want to hear!'

They all said goodbye, leaving Mandy, James and Claire to be rounded up and herded inside by Mrs McKay.

'Come into the warm!' she cried in her rolling voice. She was ready with hot chocolate and toasted teacakes, the kitchen cosy and clean. 'Now you three warm your feet and have plenty to eat,' she said. 'And then it'll be time for me to drive you into school!' She smiled; 'You've not forgotten about school, I take it!'

'No, but I wish you had!' James grumbled.

They all laughed.

'We want to have a celebration for Spike and Speedy!' Claire said. 'Don't we, Mandy?'

Mandy smiled. 'We are celebrating!' She held up her cup of hot chocolate. 'They're both safely back home!'

She paused and looked out of the window at Rosa's Refuge. James and

Claire's bright, bold crossing warning showed up well in the daylight. The 'Rosa's Refuge' sign swung to and fro. 'But, really,' she said quietly and almost to herself, 'I suppose in a way we want them not to come home.' She sighed. 'We want them to be free!'

CHAPTER NINE

A misty dawn lifted into a perfect blue day. Mandy smelt the sharp autumn smells of leaves and earth as she cycled home from school. Tonight was Bonfire Night. She saw groups of children collecting the last wood for their fires. Usually she would be one of them. But now all she could think of was hedgehogs.

She went home and quickly ate her tea, planning to meet Michelle at Rosa's Refuge. She planned to interview them for *Wildlife Ways*.

'Good luck to Tiggy and Scout!' Mr Hope called out from the surgery.

'Thanks!' Mandy looked in on him

before she set off. 'I'll probably stay on for Claire's bonfire after we've tracked Tiggy and Scout.'

'OK, take care!' he said.

As she cycled, she told herself everything would be fine again. Spike and Speedy had survived their first night, so why not Tiggy and Scout? Being hand reared obviously hadn't spoiled their chances of living wild again.

But Tiggy was so small and clumsy, she thought. Maybe she would need more protection than the others. She shook her head crossly, and told herself not to fuss. Simon and Michelle must think Tiggy was strong enough to cope. Tonight meant freedom for two more baby hedgehogs!

Michelle had already asked Mrs McKay if they could use her kitchen for the interview, so Mandy went into the lovely warm house to join James and Claire.

'Don't let the recorder put you off,' Michelle told Mandy. 'Just talk normally to me about how you rescued Rosa and then decided to set up a refuge, OK?' She held the slim machine in Mandy's direction and pressed some buttons.

Mandy swallowed hard. 'Well, I was very lucky because my mother and father are both vets at Animal Ark,' she began. 'So I knew we would be able to mend Rosa's broken leg. But I was very worried about her babies!' The story flowed as she recalled every moment of that dramatic time.

Michelle listened intently to Mandy and only rarely interrupted. Her silver earrings swung as she nodded her head. She smiled Mandy through each stage of the story.

'And once you'd established a feeding pattern for these young hedgehogs, were you ever tempted to make pets of them?' she asked.

'Oh, yes!' Mandy glanced at Claire and confessed. 'We would love to have kept them! They're beautiful animals, and people think they make sweet pets. You can feed them, and they'll come when you call,' she said.

'But?'

'But they belong in the wild!' Mandy

124

said firmly. 'They have their own nests, and they like to wander. You mustn't try to keep them in a cage.'

She saw Claire nodding her head furiously, agreeing with every word!

'What happens if you do?' Michelle asked, putting the recorder closer to Mandy as her voice dropped.

'They fight to get out. And they usually die young!'

'Yes, so that's the idea behind Rosa's Refuge,' Michelle agreed. 'To get this whole family of hedgehogs back into the wild.' She turned the machine and spoke into it. 'Mandy Hope's hedgehog refuge is turning itself into a model experiment of its kind. As we heard, last night two of the young hedgehogs were set free, and both survived. Tonight it's the turn of the other two babies, part-reared in captivity, but now about to be released!'

Michelle pressed the stop button. 'Well done, that's great!' she said. 'You didn't sound at all nervous!'

'That's because I'm more worried about Tiggy and Scout!' Mandy confessed. She got up, anxious to start.

125

'OK, I'm with you!' Michelle said, grabbing her case of equipment. 'Let's go!'

Out in Rosa's Refuge with Simon, Claire and James, Mandy and Michelle made the hedgehogs ready. 'We need to set them off well before the bonfires get started,' Michelle said. 'Then they can be well away into the woods and fields, out of harm's way. We'll track them for the first hour or so, as before. After that, it's up to them. We'll be back in the morning, ready to check them in. OK?'

They all nodded.

Mandy was especially nervous as she took Tiggy, whose tag was now glowing green in the dusk. 'Ready?' she checked.

Michelle turned up the volume on her receiver. Tiggy's signal was a rapid double bleep, followed by a pause and then repeated. 'Ready!' she said.

Mandy lowered Tiggy to Claire's level so she could say goodbye. Then she put her on to the grass. The little hedgehog picked up her front feet one at a time, as if the wet, cold ground surprised her. But soon her nose went down to the earth and she snuffled off happily.

Safe journey! Mandy thought. The little green light headed across the garden towards the neighbour's beyond. Michelle went ahead with her radio. This time, James joined Mandy and Claire and they all followed.

Through a couple of gardens, grunting and snacking, Tiggy made her way. They began to breathe more easily. Perhaps she would be all right!

When she reached open fields, they could all stand back and take a long-distance view of her. The green light zigzagged smoothly and the bleep-bleep-pause-bleep signal was strong. Then the light rose mysteriously thirty centimetres or so into the air, bobbed and vanished!

'It's OK, I've still got the signal!' Michelle said.

'Come on!' Mandy yelled, racing ahead.

They ran across the field. Underfoot the ground grew wetter. Mandy's wellingtons sank into soggy earth.

'There's a water trough!' She pointed out the shape of an old enamelled bath, now half sunk into the ground and in use as a cattle trough in one corner of the field. 'Tiggy must have fallen in there!' she shouted.

'She'll drown!' Claire cried.

Michelle held her hand. 'Don't worry; hedgehogs can swim!' she said.

James got out his torch and shone it on to the water. And there was Tiggy's little head, nose above the surface and green light glowing, doggy-paddling gamely round the water trough!

'She can't get out!' Claire gasped.

Bleep-bleep-pause-bleep!   went Tiggy's signal. She squeaked helplessly.

'Much more of that and she will go under!' Michelle said. So Mandy quickly put on her glove and guided the little swimmer towards one smooth, sheer side of the trough. There she could put her hand underneath Tiggy's belly and lift her safely out.

'She's exhausted!' Mandy said. 'Didn't I say you were accident-prone?' she scolded. 'Now, no more midnight swims!' She put Tiggy down and watched her waggle the water drops off her body.

Michelle and James laughed. Even Claire smiled. Soon Tiggy was off again, striking out towards a ditch and disappearing into the thick tangle of nettles and brambles. Her light vanished, but her signal continued strong and clear. They breathed another sigh of relief.

'Now for Scout?' Michelle suggested.

Mandy crossed her fingers for Tiggy and nodded. 'Now for Scout!' She felt easier about him somehow. Big and bold, he was the explorer.

Still she felt a pang as they went back to Rosa's Refuge and checked Scout's signal. His was a long, uninterrupted sound. He looked as funny as the rest with his little aerial attached to the glowing tag behind his ear, and Mandy, James and Claire wished him luck too as they set him free. Scout looked up at them, his head on one side. Then he was off!

Michelle tracked straight up the garden after him. Claire, James and Mandy followed her to the gate.

'There's a car coming!' James whispered, ready to leap out.

They held their breaths. Scout edged out into the road. He ignored the dip and sway of headlights down the road. The car approached, then it slowed. The "Hedgehogs Crossing" sign shone brightly in its lights. The car stopped as Scout scuttled on.

'It works!' James yelled. The others laughed and cheered.

From inside his car, the driver nodded and gave them a thumbs-up signal. Then he drove cautiously on.

'Come on, Mandy!' Michelle said. She crossed the road, hot on Scout's trail. 'He's really getting a move on. I think he's found a run!

Mandy followed, through a field into a small group of oak trees. Scout's light was still in view, then it was gone, then back in sight! The long bleep came through strongly. All was well!

The oak wood was full of dark shadows and strange noises. Mandy wasn't surprised when Scout's light finally vanished for good behind some sturdy tree-trunk or thick undergrowth.

Old trunks of knotted wood twisted into strange, almost living shapes in the dark, and bare branches stretched like fingers into the sky. The signal grew fainter and disappeared.

'Where's he gone?' Mandy whispered.

Michelle pushed buttons on her receiver, but she couldn't bring the signal back. 'Probably behind a hedgebank. It muffles the sound, remember?'

They searched on. They climbed over fallen tree-trunks and squelched through streams. But there was no sign of Scout.

'He really has gone exploring!' Michelle said at last. 'But just think of Spike last night, off on his travels. And he turned up safe and sound!'

Mandy nodded. 'OK, let's go back.' She sighed. 'There's no point in going on looking. Scout could be well out of range by now anyway!'

With a heavy heart she trudged back to Rosa's Refuge.

*   *   *

That night Claire had her bonfire surrounded by her new friends. Mandy stood beside her as Dr McKay lit a long torch of twisted newspaper and held it against some of the dry kindling at the base of the pile. Sparks carried on the wind and took light. Flames began to lick at the wood. The fire crackled and darted into the depths of the bonfire. Soon there was a fine blaze.

Mandy breathed in the smell of woodsmoke. Now the flames shot high, carrying sparks which danced in red swirls into the dark sky. 'It's a good bonfire!' Mandy said to Claire. 'And look over there!'

She pointed along the horizon above Welford, over to High Cross Farm and the Beacon. All along the way, other fires glowed; little patches of red light on the dark hillside. It made her feel connected to those far-off gardens and the children there.

Mrs Hope came and joined them as Claire's fire began to settle and fade. She brought a special Yorkshire treat of parkin for the McKays; a cake baked by Gran, made of oats, treacle and ginger. They stood around the fire, faces aglow, munching the cake from gloved hands.

'How did it go tonight?' Mrs Hope asked Mandy. She warmed her hands at the fire.

'Fine!' Mandy did her best to sound confident. Her mother laughed at the story of Tiggy's unexpected soaking. 'I'll be glad when tonight's over though!' Mandy admitted. 'I just want to see Scout and Tiggy safely back after their first night out!'

* * *

Mandy and Michelle arrived at Rosa's Refuge first, before dawn on the Wednesday morning. The smell of smoke lingered, and the sad ashes of the previous night's bonfire. James and Claire must both have slept in after the excitement of the evening before.

'Shall I wake them?' Mandy asked Michelle.

'No, let them sleep in this morning. They deserve it!' Michelle said. 'And we have to get a move on.'

Michelle quickly tuned in her receiver for Tiggy's return and they wandered down the road in the direction of the field with the water trough. It was a grey, flat light. Nothing stirred. 'Seven-thirty a.m., Wednesday the sixth of November,' Michelle said into her recorder. 'And still no sign of either of the hedgehogs released last night.'

Mandy scanned the field. All her worry for Tiggy came flooding back. The minutes ticked by.

But then Michelle began to pick up a faint signal. 'Listen!' they said together. Soon the sound grew louder. They rushed forward in its direction through the wet grass.

'She's coming home!' Mandy said to herself. 'Even Tiggy!'

But there was another surprise in store. 'This signal is still very faint,' Michelle pointed out. 'And it fades every now and then, as if the aerial isn't working properly!'

They listened hard and at last heard the telltale snortings of a hedgehog stopping off for breakfast. 'Over here!' Mandy called.

She lifted the spiky branches of a blackberry bush. Beneath it, Tiggy foraged noisily. But since last night she'd managed to have yet another curious accident!

'What's that round her middle!' Michelle gasped. 'It looks as if she's wearing a belt!'

Mandy bent and picked Tiggy up. 'It's a plastic collar from a pack of drink cans!' she announced. They examined Tiggy carefully. 'No damage done! She must have nosed her way into some rubbish and crawled inside the ring without seeing it! Now she's stuck!'

'And she's bent her aerial,' Michelle said. 'No wonder we couldn't pick up her signal very clearly!'

In spite of themselves, they smiled at the comical sight. 'That piglet's a walking disaster!' Mandy admitted.

Michelle had to use a small penknife from her pocket to cut through the plastic ring and release Tiggy.

'Shall I put her down again?' Mandy

135

asked.

Michelle straightened the aerial then nodded. She switched on her recorder. 'Seven forty-five a.m., and the smallest hedgehog has returned!' she said. 'Tiggy came home with an interesting fashion item in the shape of a plastic belt, but otherwise unharmed! We're watching now as she wanders along the run back to Rosa's Refuge. Success number three for the young team, though the night has certainly been an eventful one!'

Mandy shook her head and smiled as Tiggy finally crept through the hedge into Claire's garden.

'Three out of four!' Michelle congratulated her. 'That's not bad!'

But Mandy wanted four out of four. 'Let's go back and track Scout from where we last saw him!' she said eagerly. Her confidence was high; Scout was always the one who could look after himself.

So they retraced their steps across the road into the small oak copse. They stood where they'd picked up Scout's last signal. Michelle turned up the volume on the receiver; they met dead silence.

'He probably went much further than any of the others,' Mandy said. 'He likes to explore. He's a wanderer!'

'We could be in for a long wait,' Michelle agreed. She went forward a few paces, testing the undergrowth with her boot. 'Was it somewhere here that we lost the green light?'

Mandy thought she recognised a fallen tree trunk and the huge, twisted bole of a tree. 'Just to the left there, I think,' she agreed.

'Ah!' Michelle paused.

'What is it?' Mandy tried not to panic. But Michelle sounded suddenly serious.

'Badger!' Michelle said. 'Here's its sett!' She pointed out a hidden tunnel, neatly dug, fairly large, surrounded by footprints and scuffed earth. She looked up at Mandy. 'This could explain things,' she warned.

Mandy shook her head. 'A badger wouldn't get Scout!' she protested. 'He'd roll up into a ball. He'd wait until the danger passed!'

137

Michelle frowned. 'Badgers have very strong front claws,' she explained. 'They can prise open a hedgehog, especially a young one.'

Mandy pushed at the bushes and ferns around the entrance to the sett. 'No,' she said. 'Scout would be able to get away!'

But Michelle had walked a few metres off, beyond the enormous oak. She stopped searching and stood up. In one hand she held a broken aerial and a small metal tag. 'Mandy!' she said gently.

Mandy felt her whole body go empty and limp. She stared at Scout's radio tag.

'There are signs of a big struggle,' Michelle said. 'The leaves are disturbed. Something pretty fierce has been going on here!'

Mandy forced herself to put one foot in front of the other to join Michelle. She gazed down at the ground and saw deep claw marks and a patch of blood on the leaves.

As Michelle put one arm around her shoulder, Mandy broke down in bitter tears!

CHAPTER TEN

Simon took Mandy home to Animal Ark. Mrs Hope listened to the news and nodded. 'We'll manage,' she said quietly. She took Mandy inside.

'Cry if you want to,' she told her. 'Here's a big box of tissues, so just go ahead!' She spoke gently, with one arm round Mandy's shoulder.

Mandy couldn't put anything into words. She just wished Scout was still alive. In her memory, she saw him clear as anything nosing out on to the lawn ahead of the rest to find that first dish of food. He was the bravest of Rosa's babies. Scout the explorer. Scout the fearless one.

'I understand,' Mrs Hope said. 'When you deal with animals it's often sad. You know that yourself, Mandy. Pets get sick and die, don't they? We never want it to happen.'

Mandy nodded through her tears. 'I remember when James's cat, Benji, died.'

'And when animals live in the wild it's dangerous. They don't all survive. They have enemies; there are all sorts of accidents that can happen!'

Gradually Mandy stopped crying. 'I do know!' she agreed.

'And I know how you're feeling,' Mrs Hope said. 'Nothing I say will actually help you stop missing little Scout. Only time will do that.' She held Mandy's head against her shoulder. 'So what do you want to do? Do you feel up to going into school?'

Mandy sniffed and sat upright. She remembered James in school, quiet and pale on the day Benji died. 'Yes, I want to go in,' she said.

Mrs Hope looked at her and nodded. 'Good. I'll sort out a lift for you. We're a bit late for you to go in by bike.' She gave Mandy one last hug. '*Wildlife Ways* is on tonight, isn't it?'

'Yes. Michelle's spending the day editing the tape,' Mandy told her. 'She has to get it ready for the broadcast.'

'That's terrific!' her mother said, smiling at her. 'I'm so proud of you, Mandy Hope!'

Before the programme came on the air, Mandy and the Operation Hedgehog team had one final task to complete. They had one more hedgehog to set free. At dusk that evening it was Rosa's turn!

Simon lifted her out of her nest-box. He asked Mandy to shine a torch on to the broken leg while he clipped away at the plaster bandage. Everyone stood around watching. Soon the leg was free. Simon felt it gently with his fingertips, then handed Rosa to Mandy. 'Feel it. It seems to be OK,' he said.

Mandy felt the injured leg. She had Rosa nestling in the gloved palm of her left hand and felt up and down the thin little leg with her right. No swellings, no bumps in the bone. 'As good as new!' she said. Rosa blinked happily and sniffed at the leather glove.

'I think so too!' Simon said.

Mandy took a deep breath. 'So, we're ready!' She put Rosa down on the lawn of Rosa's Refuge.

As she stepped back, she felt Claire come up and quietly take her hand.

Rosa settled on to the wet grass. Her nose twitched. She made a short run up the lawn, stopped, shunted sideways, then made a few circular runs for practice.

'No problem with the leg!' James laughed.

They all followed as Rosa trotted happily to the gate, smelling her way towards old, familiar runs. She scuttled through the gate and ambled down the roadside, past the 'Hedgehogs Crossing' sign towards James's garden gate. Then she made a sharp left turn up his path.

'Not again!' Mandy cried. Rosa was making straight for James's hallway.

'This is where we started!' James laughed. 'It's OK; Blackie's safe in the back of the house,' he promised.

They watched in disbelief as Rosa sniffed her way up the front step.

'Oh, no, your dad!' Mandy cried again. Mr Hunter had opened the front door to see what all the noise was about. Blackie scrabbled furiously against the kitchen door.

'Watch out, Dad!' James yelled.

Mr Hunter stood, legs wide apart, in his stockinged feet. They all groaned as Rosa nipped in between his legs, straight into the hall!

'Don't move!' Mandy warned.

Mr Hunter looked aghast.

Rosa sniffed the doormat and zigzagged between his legs. 'Oh, look, she's coming back!' Mandy cried in relief this time, as Rosa half leapt, half rolled back down the step on to the path.

Thank heavens! They all sighed. Mr Hunter stood there, dumbfounded, shaking his head.

Two cars came down the lane, headlights catching the hedges and walls, as Rosa muddled along happily between flower-beds and garden seats in James's garden. Both cars slowed down when they saw the 'Hedgehogs Crossing' sign, and both drove slowly on down the road.

Rosa took not a bit of notice. She didn't venture back on to the road, but chose a path along the grass verge, under James and Claire's sign, back towards Rosa's Refuge. Mandy and her group tramped up the Hunters' path, out on to the road, and found her again. She was nosing her way into a feeding station to find her evening meal.

They waited while she munched and snorted.

'Look over there!' Claire pointed to a strange light glowing under their shed. 'I think it's Tiggy!'

'It is!' Mandy said. She recognised the wobbly walk.

Tiggy trotted forward as Rosa finished feeding. The two hedgehogs greeted each other with quiet, contented snuffles.

'I think she can get along without this now!' Simon said, as he went over and bent quickly to unclip the glowing tag and aerial. He smiled at Mandy.

Soon two more lights came floating out of the deepest shadows. Spike and Speedy had returned to greet their mother. When Simon had carefully removed their radio tags too, the family could get on with its reunion. Rosa circled her three children. She nosed each one in turn and circled them again. Then she retreated to the edge of the lawn. She watched as first Speedy, then Spike and Tiggy set off on their night's adventure.

Slow old Guy snorted loudly from the hedge to call Speedy, and they set off across the road as usual. Tiggy wobbled from lawn to path, then vanished into another hedge. A snort or two told them she was happily eating slugs for supper! Spike, minding his own business, cut behind the shed and headed for a new dark corner to explore. Soon all three were gone.

Mandy sighed. She watched Rosa turn and begin to root around under a tree. She spiked dead leaves on to her spines by rummaging deep into a raked pile of them.

'Nest building!' Simon told them excitedly.

'Where?' James asked. 'Does this mean she'll choose somewhere close by to hibernate?'

Simon nodded, then told them to

watch closely. 'She's getting ready for a long winter's sleep!' he said, looking at his watch. 'And don't I wish it was me!'

Mandy smiled. If Rosa was getting ready to hibernate in Rosa's Refuge, it would be one more triumph for them! And soon Rosa, under her collection of dead leaves and grass, trotted back out on to the lawn.

'She looks like a moving compost heap!' James whispered.

'She's heading for her own nest-box!' Claire said. 'I think she's going to spend the winter in your box, James!'

Rosa busily snorted her way towards the box under the beech tree, carrying her winter bedding with her. She disappeared straight down the tunnel and didn't come out. They waited, but there was no sign of her; only the quiet creaking of the 'Rosa's Refuge' sign as it swung in the cold night wind.

*   *   *

Rosa's babies had gone foraging into the night—to eat, to build nests, to hibernate. Rosa herself had chosen

146

lodgings closer to home. At last, Mandy, James, Claire and Simon could go in out of the cold.

They went into Claire's kitchen, where the radio was already turned on. Dr McKay had tuned it into the right station. 'Any time now,' he announced. 'Are you sure you're all ready for instant stardom?'

Mandy gave an embarrassed grin and went to sit in a far corner. She was trying to keep an eye on the comings and goings out in Rosa's Refuge. But the kitchen light against the dark sky turned the window into a mirror. She saw only her own reflection; blonde hair damp from the mist, her eyes dark and wide. She gave up and turned to face James and Claire. The music played for the start of *Wildlife Ways*.

Michelle's voice introduced itself. They sat and grinned at one another. 'We know her!' Claire said proudly. 'She's our friend and she's on the radio!'

Mandy agreed. How strange it was to hear someone you knew well.

'Shh!' Mrs McKay said. But really

she looked as excited as the rest.

They heard Michelle describe the aims of Rosa's Refuge. And then there was Mandy's own voice, sounding to her like someone else entirely! 'That's not me!' she cried. She felt herself blush bright red.

'It is! Shh!' they all said.

'This week saw the greatest triumph for the Welford team!' Michelle went on. 'On Monday and Tuesday of this week, they managed to rehabilitate the hedgehogs back into the wild!'

They sat and listened to the story of Spike and Speedy's release and of their safe return. They listened to the account of the second night; Tiggy and Scout's journey to freedom. Michelle described how little Tiggy survived. 'Sadly, Scout was not so lucky,' she said. 'When he failed to return to Rosa's Refuge this morning, Mandy and I set out to search the area where we'd last seen him. We found clear signs of a fatal struggle with a badger.'

Tears were in all their eyes as they listened.

But Michelle went on to round off

her report.

'Scout's death in no way lessens the success of the project,' she said firmly. 'Rosa's Refuge is a brilliant plan to help wildlife. It has been put into operation by a group of dedicated animal lovers. We think it is one of the best schemes for rescuing and rehabilitating hedgehogs that we have ever come across!'

She paused before signing off. 'Here on *Wildlife Ways* we wish Rosa's Refuge well. Long may it continue to help injured and underweight hedgehogs recover their strength and their ability to survive in the wild!'

Mandy looked proudly at her friends. Her eyes shone with happiness. 'Well?' she asked Claire.

Claire thought long and hard. 'Guy's still here. And Rosa's here!' she said. 'And any other hedgehogs who need a home can come into my garden and be looked after by me for as long as they like!'

Mandy looked towards Dr and Mrs McKay.

'Of course they can!' they both

agreed. 'Rosa's Refuge is open for business!'

Finally Mandy looked at James in perfect contentment. 'Then long may it continue!' she said.